The Weight

of

Staying Alive

The Weight of Staying Alive

By: Blake Collins

The Weight of Staying Alive

ISBN: 979-8-9936801-3-2

Cover design by Blake Collins

Interior design by Blake Collins

Published by Blake Collins

Idaho Falls, Idaho

Printed in the United States of America

First Printing, 2026

To my five children—

May you never stop believing in the life you want.

May you never shrink your dreams to fit someone else's expectations.

And when the road gets tough, keep walking anyway.

I'll be cheering for you every step.

"I just want to live.

I want to be alive."

— *It's Kind of a Funny Story*

Table of Contents

Chapter 1 – The Final Birthday

How would you spend your birthday if you knew you wouldn't see your next?

I am sitting at the table, watching my dad carefully light the fifteen candles on my cake. He does it slowly, like if he goes too fast something might go wrong. The flames flicker and sway, reflecting in the thin layer of frosting like tiny orange stars.

Balloons are tied to the back of my chair, squeaking softly every time someone walks past. They bump gently against my shoulders, as if they are trying to remind me I am supposed to be celebrating. The stack of wrapped presents at the edge of the table looks bright and cheerful and completely out of place. It feels like it belongs to someone else's birthday.

The cake smells too sweet. Chocolate and sugar hang heavy in the air, thick enough to make my stomach roll. My mom stands across from me, already holding her phone up, the little red recording light blinking.

"Make a wish," she says, forcing a brightness into her voice. "Come on, honey. Big breath."

I try. I really do. I pull in what air I can, my chest tightening as I lean forward. The heat from the candles presses against my face. I blow, and the flames go out all at once, but the effort sends a wave of dizziness through me so strong I have to grip the edge of the table to keep myself upright.

My mom laughs a little too loudly. "There we go," she says. "See. Still got it."

My dad claps once, soft and careful. "Fifteen," he says. "That is a big one, buddy."

He slices the cake and sets the first piece in front of me. A thick line of frosting slides down the side as he moves it. I take my fork and poke at it, lifting a small bite to my mouth. The sweetness hits my tongue like a wall. It is too rich, too heavy, and my stomach turns instantly.

I swallow hard.

"What is wrong, sweetheart?" my mom asks, lowering her phone. "Are you feeling okay?"

"My stomach isn't great, and my head is killing me," I say. My voice comes out thinner than I expect, like it is already tired of holding itself together.

She steps closer, worry instantly replacing the forced smile. "Do you want to open your presents?" she asks, desperate for something that might pull me back into the moment. "Maybe that will help."

"I think I am going to go lie down for a bit," I tell her. "I am beat."

My dad's eyes flicker toward me, just for a second. It isn't disappointment. It is something worse. It is the quiet grief of watching a birthday turn into something small and fragile. He knows what this should look like. He knows I should be at the trampoline park with my friends from the football team, laughing too loud and sweating through my jersey. I should be ripping into my presents, hyped about new video games and gear he worked overtime to buy.

Instead, I am dragging myself away from the table, exhausted by something as simple as sitting upright.

Ever since mid-June, my energy has been gone. Not tired, but drained. The migraines. The dizzy spells. The moments where everything tilts and goes black. They have become a part of my everyday life, as normal as brushing my teeth used to be.

The first time I passed out, I woke up in a hospital bed and spent three days there.

MRIs. X rays. Blood tests. Everyone searching. No one finding anything.

The symptoms kept getting worse. And eventually I had to quit the football team.

I still remember standing on the field that last day, helmet tucked under my arm, watching my teammates run drills without me. The sound of pads colliding echoed through the air, sharp and familiar. My jersey hung loose on my shoulders, suddenly too big, like it belonged to a version of me that was already gone. Coach clapped me on the back and told me to focus on getting better, but we both knew what that really meant.

Letting go of the sport I loved was hard enough. Watching my friends drift away afterward has been even harder.

It feels like as I leave that part of my life behind, they are leaving me behind too.

It has been four months now. The symptoms are getting worse. Happening more often. Closing in on me.

I am dying, and I know it.

This is the last year of my life.

My last birthday.

My last Thanksgiving.

My last Christmas.

My last everything.

I have had to accept a future I will never live. I will not go to college. I will not get married. I will not have kids. I will not grow into the person I always imagined I would become. The truth is bleak and heavy. I will probably be gone before I even get the chance to drive a car.

I walk through the living room and down the hall into my cool, dark bedroom. I don't bother turning on the lights. The shadows feel easier. My trophies still line the shelf above my desk. My football posters still hang crooked on the walls. It all looks like it is waiting for someone who might not come back.

I collapse onto my bed, pulling the blanket up to my chin. The fabric smells faintly like laundry soap and something older, something that feels like home. My head throbs in slow, angry pulses behind my eyes.

I close my eyes, knowing it is only 5:30.

I fall asleep anyway.

A moment later, voices drift through the hallway.

My mom's voice. Sharp. Trembling.

A faint beeping fills the room, steady and unnerving.

"He is getting worse, doctor. There has to be a cause. The migraines, the headaches," she pleads. "They are controlling his life."

"Ma'am, I understand," the doctor says, calm and distant. "We are doing everything we can."

"All you can isn't enough," she snaps. "What kind of life is this? Hooked up to machines, in and out of hospitals? He is just a kid."

The voices blur, growing louder, then softer, like they are underwater.

I try to call out. I try to tell her I am here, that I am listening, that I am not gone yet.

But no sound leaves my mouth.

And then everything goes quiet.

Chapter 2 – The Things They Don't Say

When I wake up, the room is dark and my head feels like it is wrapped in thick cotton. The world comes back in pieces. The ceiling first. The faint glow of streetlight through my curtains. The dull ache behind my eyes that never really leaves anymore.

I blink slowly, trying to remember where I am. My bed. My room. Home. It feels strange to be here when so much of my life has been happening in hospitals lately. My throat is dry. My limbs feel heavy, like gravity has decided to press down harder on me than it does on everyone else.

Then I hear it.

Voices drifting down the hallway.

Not echoing this time. Not warped and distorted like in the dream I just crawled out of.

Real.

I stay still, barely breathing, listening.

My mom's voice carries first, sharp and trembling. "He isn't getting better, Michael. You saw him at the table. He could barely sit up."

"He was just tired," my dad says, trying to keep his voice low, but the strain still slips through. "He has been through a lot lately. But he is fine."

"He isn't fine," she snaps back. "You don't pass out for no reason. You don't get migraines that make you sick to your stomach. Something is wrong."

A drawer slams somewhere down the hall. The sound makes me flinch even though I know it isn't close to me.

"We have seen every specialist they recommended," my dad says. "Every test has come back clean. What else do you want me to do? Invent an illness?"

For a moment there is only silence. It stretches out, thick and uncomfortable, like no one knows how to move past it.

Then my mom's voice breaks.

"I just want my son back."

The words hit me harder than anything she has said so far.

I press my lips together, afraid that if I breathe too loudly, they will hear me and stop talking. My chest feels tight. Not from pain, but from something deeper. Something colder.

I push myself upright slowly, waiting for the dizziness to pass. My head spins anyway, but I force myself to my feet. The carpet is soft under my toes as I move toward the door. I have to brace my hand against the wall, steadying myself as I reach the hallway.

Their voices stop the second I step out.

Both of them turn toward me. My mom's eyes are red and swollen. My dad's jaw is tight, the muscles there twitching like he is biting back something he does not want to say.

"Hey," I say quietly. My voice feels too small in the space between us. "I… I think I feel a little better."

My mom rushes toward me. "Sweetheart, you should still be resting."

"I know." I swallow. "But maybe I could open my presents now. If that is okay."

There is a beat of hesitation. A look passes between them that I am not supposed to see. Fear and hope tangled together.

Then my dad nods.

"Yeah," he says, forcing a smile. "Yeah, bud. Of course."

And just like that, the argument disappears into the walls. It is like someone hit a switch and turned it off. We are no longer a family falling apart. We are a normal family about to open birthday presents.

At least that is what we pretend.

We all know better.

Not anymore.

I sit on the couch, sinking into the cushions like my body weighs more than it should. My dad carries the stack of presents over and sets them carefully on the coffee table in front of me. It is the only way my mom agreed to let me out of my room.

I try to smile. It feels like stretching a muscle that has not been used in a long time.

My dad lowers himself onto the edge of the table, watching me with the same look he used to have when I was a little kid. Back when new video games or a football helmet could light up my whole world. Now he watches me like he is hoping that version of me is still in there somewhere.

I know he is more excited about these gifts than I am.

As I look at the bright paper and shiny bows, a strange heaviness settles in my chest.

What will happen to all this stuff once I am gone?

Will my room stay exactly the way I leave it, frozen in time like some kind of museum?

Will anyone even go in there at all?

The thought makes my stomach twist.

I tear into the first gift. The paper rips loudly in the quiet room. Inside is a new copy of Madden, Joe Burrow on the cover after winning MVP last season. My dad's eyes light up as he waits for my reaction.

"Thanks," I say, managing a small smile.

"Once you are feeling better," he says gently, "we will get back to our weekly matchups. I have been practicing."

I nod, even though something about that makes my chest ache. Like he is talking about a future I am not sure I get to have.

The next few presents are practical things. Socks. Underwear. A couple of shirts. A pair of jeans. I thank them both and tell them how much I appreciate it all, even though opening clothes for a future I might not reach feels heavier than it should.

My mom stands off to the side, quietly crying, her phone lifted again to take pictures. I can tell she is trying to memorize this moment. Like she is afraid there will not be many more.

My dad leans down and kisses my forehead. His hand lingers there just a little too long.

“I should probably head to bed,” I say, pushing myself up slowly. “I have got school tomorrow. And you know how wiped out I get after a full day.”

They both nod. Neither of them says anything.

We are all pretending I will wake up tomorrow and be just another kid going to high school.

But we all know better.

Chapter 3 – What if I'm Right

When I wake up, the first thing I feel is the pounding.

Not a normal headache. This one is deep and heavy, like someone wedged a steel rod behind my eyes and keeps tapping it with a hammer. It pulses in time with my heartbeat, steady and cruel, like it has been waiting for me to open my eyes just so it can remind me it is still here.

I try sitting up.

Big mistake.

The room tilts so hard I have to grab the edge of my mattress to keep from sliding off. My stomach flips, and for a second I think I might actually throw up right there on my sheets. My throat tightens. Sweat prickles at the back of my neck. The air feels too thin, like it isn't doing its job.

Great.

Another morning starting the exact same way.

I close my eyes and breathe slowly. One inhale. One exhale. Another. I count them in my head like counting can keep my body from betraying me. My hands stay clenched in the blanket, fingers white, because letting go feels like permission to fall.

This was not how my days used to begin.

I used to wake up to my alarm, annoyed but normal. I used to check my phone and see a string of texts from teammates about practice, or a message from someone asking if I wanted to meet up before first period. I used to complain about being tired in the way healthy people complain, like it was something sleep could fix.

Now all I wake up to is pain.

And the worst part is I don't even question it anymore.

This is just my life now.

After a minute, the spinning eases into something duller. Not gone. Just quiet enough to move. I swing my legs over the side of the bed slowly and wait to see if the floor will tilt again. My feet hit the carpet and feel disconnected from the rest of me, like they belong to someone else.

I stand carefully.

My balance wobbles, but I stay upright. My stomach sways with the motion and I swallow hard, forcing it down. The air in my room is cool, but my skin still feels hot, like I am running a fever I cannot prove.

I make it to the doorway. One hand trails the wall as I move down the hallway, palm dragging along the paint like I am trying to anchor myself to something solid.

The house is quiet except for the kitchen. I can hear the soft clink of dishes, the low hum of the coffee maker, and the faint rustle of a lunch bag opening and closing.

Mom is at the counter packing lunches. She looks up the second she hears me, and her face tightens with worry.

"You don't look good," she says softly.

"I am fine," I lie.

I always lie.

It is easier than telling the truth, and it is definitely easier than watching her panic. It is easier than watching her eyes fill, easier than hearing her voice go sharp and scared. It is easier than giving her another reason to call the hospital, another reason to beg for answers nobody seems able to give.

Dad glances over from the coffee maker. He is holding his mug like it is the only thing keeping him steady.

"He probably just didn't sleep well," he says, shrugging it off like usual. "He will be okay once he gets moving."

His voice is calm, but his eyes don't match it. He watches me too closely, like he is trying to memorize the way I am standing. Like he is waiting for the exact second I wobble.

Mom does not argue, but the way she watches me makes my skin itch. She is looking for signs. Pale face. Glassy eyes. The tiny sway of my shoulders. She is watching like she is waiting for me to collapse right there on the kitchen tile.

I sit at the table, but it isn't really sitting. It is more like lowering myself carefully so I don't trigger another dizzy spell. The overhead light feels too bright, sharp enough to stab. The clatter of dishes sounds like someone banging metal pans inside my skull.

Mom slides a plate of toast in front of me.

"Try to eat something," she says.

I nod and take one bite. The bread tastes like cardboard. My stomach clenches in protest. I chew slowly, forcing it down, then take a sip of water and swallow hard.

The second bite does not happen.

I set the toast down and stare at it like it might start making sense if I look long enough.

Dad flips through his phone like he is reading headlines, but I know he isn't. He keeps glancing up. Keeps checking.

Mom moves around the kitchen too quickly, doing unnecessary things like wiping a counter that is already clean, rinsing a cup that is already rinsed. She is trying to act normal, but everything she does is tense.

"You sure you are okay to go?" she asks.

"I have to," I say.

That is the other lie. The one that feels like a rule.

If I don't go to school, I lose another piece of my life.

If I stay home, it confirms what I already believe.

That I am not getting better.

That I am running out of time.

Dad clears his throat. "We will take it easy today," he says, like he is talking to a kid with a sprained ankle.

I nod, like that solves anything.

By the time we pull up to school, I already feel wiped out. Completely drained. And the day has not even started.

Mom keeps her hands tight on the steering wheel after she parks. She does not immediately unlock the doors. She just sits there, staring at the building like it is a place she is sending me into without armor.

"You call if you feel weird," she says.

"I always feel weird," I mutter.

She flinches anyway.

Dad leans forward from the passenger seat. "Just take it slow," he says. "No hero stuff."

I want to tell him I am not trying to be a hero. I am just trying to get through the day without blacking out in front of everyone again.

Instead, I nod, because that is what they need.

I step out of the car. The air is cold, and it hits my lungs like a slap. For a second it almost helps. It wakes something up inside me. But the light is too bright and the noise is already too loud, and my head throbs harder as I walk toward the doors.

Inside the building, everything feels amplified.

Lockers slam. Shoes squeak against the tile. Someone laughs too loudly. The fluorescent lights buzz overhead like a swarm of insects. My head pulses with every sound.

I keep my head low. I don't want anyone asking questions or telling me I look sick. I already know I do. I can feel it in the way people hesitate when they see me. The way their eyes flicker over my face, quick and worried. The way they decide not to speak.

People don't talk to me much anymore anyway.

At first, they were supportive.

"Feel better, man."

"Text me if you need anything."

"You will be back on the field in no time."

Then the weeks dragged into months. The messages got fewer. Then they stopped.

Now they wave from a distance. They give me the same look you give someone at a funeral. Like they don't know what to say, so they say nothing.

Teachers treat me differently too.

They don't say it out loud, but I can tell.

Late assignments get "don't worry about it."

Missed homework gets a quiet nod instead of a lecture.

I do the bare minimum, and somehow it is enough.

Part of me hates it.

Part of me is relieved.

Most of me is just too exhausted to care.

Halfway to first period, a spike of pain shoots through my skull so suddenly I have to stop walking. It is sharp and immediate, like lightning inside my brain. My vision blurs at the edges, like someone smeared Vaseline over my eyes. The hallway tilts slightly, not enough to drop me, but enough to scare me.

I duck into the nearest bathroom before anyone can notice.

Inside, the fluorescent lights are worse. They bounce off the mirrors and the white tile, harsh and unforgiving. My stomach flips again. I push into a stall and lower myself onto the closed toilet lid, elbows on my knees, head in my hands.

I breathe in slowly.

Breathe out.

The pounding keeps going.

I pull my phone from my pocket with shaky hands.

I know I should not.

I know exactly what I will see.

But fear is louder than logic.

I type in my symptoms again. Migraines. Dizziness. Fainting. Nausea. My fingers hesitate over the search button like I am about to press something that will change my life.

Then I do it anyway.

The results flash onto the screen.

Brain tumor.

Malignant.

Progressive symptoms.

Fatal if untreated.

My stomach drops.

I scroll, even though I already know what it will say. I read the words like I am reading my own obituary.

Headaches that worsen over time.

Nausea and vomiting.

Dizziness.

Balance issues.

Fainting.

Vision changes.

I swallow hard.

Every symptom matches.

Every description lines up.

Every warning feels like it is aimed straight at me.

The doctors have not found anything.

Yet.

That is the word that keeps repeating in my head.

Yet.

Because symptoms don't lie. Bodies don't do this for no reason. People don't collapse in hallways for fun. They don't live with a skull that feels like it is cracking open from the inside and then get told their scans are clean.

Something inside me is getting worse.

Faster.

Stronger.

And I cannot shake the feeling that whatever is growing in my head has been there all along. Hiding. Waiting. Spreading in places the machines cannot see.

The screen blurs as my eyes sting, and a cold certainty settles in my chest.

What if this really is the beginning of the end?

What if I don't make it to sixteen?

What if this isn't fear lying to me at all?

What if I am right?

I shove my phone back into my pocket, like hiding it will hide the thought too. My throat feels tight. I stand on shaky legs and splash cold water onto my face, hoping it will shock my body into acting normal.

It does not.

The fear stays. The shaking does not stop.

I stare at myself in the mirror for a second. My face looks pale. My eyes look too big. Too tired. The person looking back at me does not look like a fifteen-year-old who should be worried about homework and football games and who is taking who to homecoming.

He looks like someone waiting for bad news.

I wipe my hands on my jeans and step out of the bathroom.

The hallway feels too bright. The buzzing lights. The echoing footsteps. The lockers slamming like thunder. My head throbs in time with every noise.

I try to breathe through it.

Pretend I am normal.

Pretend I am fine.

But the floor shifts under me.

I blink hard. Once. Twice. The world drags sideways like someone pulled the rug out from beneath my feet. A wave of dizziness hits so fast my stomach lurches.

I reach for the wall to steady myself, but my fingers barely register the metal. They feel numb. Floating. Like my hands are not fully connected to my body.

Someone says my name.

"Rett?"

Maybe a friend. Maybe a teacher. The sound stretches and warps, like it is coming from the end of a tunnel.

I take a step forward.

The hallway tilts again.

My stomach drops.

My knees buckle.

I try to grab the locker. I miss.

For a split second, I have time to think one clear, terrified thought.

This is it.

Then everything goes black.

Chapter 4 – Clean

The next thing I know, there are voices.

Sharp, urgent voices I don't recognize. The words cut through the dark like someone is trying to pull me up by the collar.

"He is coming around."

"Stay with us, okay? Can you hear me?"

My eyelids flutter. My head throbs so hard it feels like the world is beating against my skull from the inside. For a second I don't know where I am. I only know the pain. I only know the weight pressing behind my eyes, the sick roll in my stomach, and the distant, steady sound of something beeping.

I try to move.

My body does not respond the way it should.

Something is wrapped around my arm. Something tight and plastic. A dull ache pulses at my elbow.

When my eyes finally open, the ceiling comes into focus in slow pieces. White tiles. Soft fluorescent lights. The kind of bright that is supposed to be calming, but still stabs.

Hospital.

The realization lands like a punch.

My mouth is dry, like I have been breathing through sand. My tongue feels thick. I swallow and it hurts.

Someone is holding my hand.

My mom.

Her fingers are wrapped around mine so tightly it almost hurts, like she is afraid if she lets go, I will disappear. Her face is streaked with tears. Her hair is pulled back like she did it in a rush, and there is a red mark on her cheek like she has been wiping her face too hard.

Dad is hovering behind her, trying to look calm and absolutely failing. His arms are crossed, but one hand keeps flexing like he does not know what to do with it. His eyes are bloodshot. His jaw works as if he is grinding his teeth.

A doctor stands at the foot of my bed, flipping through a chart with a crease between his eyebrows.

"You fainted at school," he says. His voice is professional, controlled, like he has said these words a thousand times. "Your teachers said you were disoriented beforehand. We ran bloodwork, scans, neurological assessments. So far, nothing concerning has shown up."

Nothing concerning.

My mom's breath catches. Her grip tightens.

"Nothing?" she says, like she thinks she misheard him. "He has been having headaches, dizziness, nausea. It has been weeks of this. Months."

The doctor nods slowly, cautious. "We don't have a clear cause yet. But we are going to keep looking."

I stare at the blanket covering my legs.

So, they still cannot find it.

Whatever this thing is inside me, whatever is getting worse. They have not seen it.

Yet.

The word flares in my head like a warning sign.

Yet.

Because I know what comes after yet. Yet means not today. Yet means maybe tomorrow. Yet means it is still there, hiding. Growing. Waiting.

And for the first time since all of this started, the fear does not whisper.

It screams.

I try to remember the hallway. I try to remember the moment before everything went black. There are flashes. Buzzing lights. The slam of lockers. Someone saying my name. A hand reaching for me too late. My knees giving out like my body decided to shut down without asking permission.

I can almost hear it again, the rushing sound in my ears, like I was being pulled underwater.

Then nothing.

My mom strokes my knuckles with her thumb. “You scared me,” she whispers. Her voice cracks. She tries to smile but it does not work. “Do you hear me? You scared me so bad.”

“I am sorry,” I manage, though it makes no sense to apologize for collapsing.

Dad leans forward. “How bad is the headache?” he asks.

“Bad,” I say. It is the only honest word I have.

The doctor nods and steps closer. “We are going to treat the pain. We are also going to keep you for observation.”

Observation.

Like I am a problem they cannot solve, so they are going to watch me until I either get better or prove them right.

A nurse appears at my side, checking the IV line, speaking quietly to the doctor. I feel a cool pressure as something slides into my vein. It is cold and numbing, like relief being poured into me.

The pounding in my skull loosens its grip slowly. Not gone, but quieter. The kind of quiet that makes me realize how loud it was before. My eyelids grow heavy.

I try to fight it.

I don’t want to sleep in case something happens while I am gone.

But my body wins.

It always does.

I slip under before I even realize I have let go.

—

When I wake again, it feels like I am floating.

Not in a peaceful way. More like my whole body is buzzing, weightless, detached, like someone turned the volume down on reality but left the fear behind. The lights above me blur around the edges. I cannot tell if it is the drugs, the exhaustion, or whatever is happening inside my head.

I blink a few times, trying to anchor myself. The room feels hollowed out and too quiet, like I stepped into another version of it while I was gone.

My mom is asleep in the chair across from me. She is curled awkwardly on one side, her arm tucked beneath her cheek. Her shoes are still on. Her jacket has not moved. She must have sat down "just for a minute" and stayed there.

Or however long it has been.

Her face looks softer in sleep. Younger. But there is worry carved into the corners of her eyes, deep enough that rest cannot erase it. Seeing it hurts more than the headache ever could.

I shift slightly. The blanket rustles. My throat feels like paper when I whisper, "Mom?"

She does not stir.

A monitor hums quietly beside me, steady and calm.

Two things I definitely am not.

The relief from the medicine is still there, but it feels thin now. Like a sheet over something broken. My head is tender again, sore in a way that reminds me the relief is borrowed. Manufactured. Temporary.

Across the room, the door clicks softly.

A nurse slips inside with practiced quiet, checks the monitor, then glances at me.

"Oh," she whispers, careful not to wake my mom. "Hey. You are awake."

I nod.

"How is the pain now?"

I swallow, tasting metallic dryness. "Better," I say, but the word feels fragile.

She nods like she expected that answer. "Good. We will keep an eye on it." She adjusts something at the foot of the bed, then hesitates, like she is choosing her next words.

"Your scans came back clean again," she says gently.

Clean.

Again.

The word sinks like a stone in my stomach.

Clean means nothing is wrong. Clean means I should be fine. Clean means I should not be here. Clean means I should not have blacked out on the tile floor at school. Clean means my mom should not be sleeping in a chair like she is bracing for a disaster.

Clean means I am invisible to the machines.

And that is somehow worse.

If something showed up, at least it would have a name. At least it would be real on paper. At least it would be something doctors could point to and fight.

But clean means it is still a mystery.

Clean means they can keep telling me they don't know.

Clean means I have to keep living like this, trapped between terror and uncertainty, waking up every day waiting for my body to do something worse.

"If everything is clean," I whisper before I can stop myself, "why do I feel like I am falling apart?"

The nurse's face softens. She does not have an answer. I can see it in her eyes. She reaches out and smooths the blanket near my feet, a small gesture that feels like apology.

"The doctor will be in soon to talk with you," she says quietly. "Try to rest, okay? You have had a rough day."

Rough day.

Yeah. Something like that.

She slips back toward the door and closes it softly behind her.

I stare at my mom again, the way she holds herself even in sleep, like she is bracing for whatever comes next. Like she cannot afford to relax because the second she does, something will happen.

I sink deeper into the pillow and try to steady my breathing.

In.

Out.

In.

Out.

The buzzing from the medicine is wearing off. The reality underneath is starting to claw its way back.

And even though the tests say nothing is wrong, my body tells a different story. A louder one.

Something is happening.

Something they cannot see.

And it terrifies me.

Sleep drags me under again.

It isn't peaceful. It is more like slipping beneath a heavy current. I am too tired to fight, too scared to want to stay awake. The last thing I remember is the ache pulsing behind my eyes and the thought that maybe tomorrow will be worse.

I don't know how long I am out.

But the next thing I hear is a soft knock at the door.

For a moment, I don't move. The air feels different.

Lighter.

Warm sunlight spills across my blanket, stretching toward me like it is trying to pull me back to the surface. My brain takes a few slow seconds to catch up.

Another knock. Gentle. Patient.

I push myself upright, blinking at the brightness. My head does not feel great, but it isn't the crushing weight from before. I am caught somewhere between relief and suspicion when the door creaks open.

The room is bright in a way that makes everything look sharper. White walls. Silver equipment. The paper beneath me crinkles as I shift, still wrapped in the fog of sleep.

My mom is out in the hallway talking quietly with someone, her voice low and tired. I cannot hear the words, but I can hear the edge of panic underneath them.

Dad is nowhere in sight.

I stare at the ceiling for a second, steadying myself, when I realize someone is standing in the doorway.

A man in his mid-thirties, maybe. Badge clipped to his shirt, but no scrubs. Just a polo and khakis. He looks too normal for this place. Too much like someone you would see at a school meeting or a grocery store, not in a room full of machines.

"Hey," he says gently. "Mind if I come in?"

I lift one shoulder in a shrug. It could mean yes. It could mean no. It does not matter.

He steps inside like he is walking into a living room instead of a hospital room. His hands are tucked loosely in his pockets. He does not look at the monitors. He does not glance at the chart. He looks at me.

That alone makes my stomach tighten.

"So," he begins, voice steady, "my job here is to help kids and teens deal with all the hospital stuff."

He gestures around the room like it is casual.

"Procedures. Tests. Being stuck here when you would rather be anywhere else. I try to make this whole situation a little less awful."

I say nothing.

The silence isn't a choice. It is all I have.

He does not flinch.

"I am what is called a Child Life Specialist," he continues. "Which is just a fancy way of saying I help you cope with everything going on."

There is a softness in his expression. No pity. No forced cheer. Just someone trying to meet me where I am.

"I would introduce myself," he says, "but you don't seem up for small talk."

Something in my chest tightens at that. Not because he is wrong, but because he said it like it was allowed. Like I didn't have to perform being okay for him.

I turn my head slightly toward the window, staring at the slice of sky beyond the glass. It looks unfairly normal. Blue. Bright. Like the world has not changed at all.

He nods, like he understands.

"No pressure," he says quietly. "I just wanted to check in. Make sure you knew you have got someone on your side while you are here."

He steps back toward the doorway, leaving the air around me a little less crowded.

"I will swing by again later," he adds. "If you feel like talking then, great. If not, that is okay too."

He slips into the hallway, leaving the door half open behind him.

Mom returns a moment later, wiping at her eyes, asking if I need water.

But I barely hear her.

I am still staring at the door.

Because for some reason I cannot explain, that guy, the specialist, his presence felt different.

Not comforting. Not yet.

Not someone I trust.

But also, not someone who treated me like a diagnosis, or a burden, or a fragile piece of glass.

He didn't talk around me. He didn't look through me.

He looked at me like I was still a person.

And in this place, that counts for more than it probably should.

Chapter 5 – More Than a Bad Day

Silence stretches between me and Mom. Machines hum softly. The fluorescent light above my bed flickers once, like it is trying to decide whether to keep working or give up.

The IV tugs at my arm when I shift. It isn't painful, just uncomfortable enough to remind me that I am not really free to move the way I want to. The air smells like disinfectant and plastic and something faintly sour, like sickness that never fully leaves. The sheets feel stiff under my fingers, not soft like home.

"Maybe you should rest," Mom says finally.

"I am tired of resting," I mutter.

She gives me that look, the one that is half worry and half I don't know how to fix this. It makes my chest ache in a different way.

"I just want to stand up," I say. "Move. I feel okay right now."

That part is true. For the moment, at least.

That is the worst thing about all of this. It comes in waves.

There are stretches where I feel almost normal, headache hovering in the background, dizziness down to a dull wobble. My body pretends everything is fine, like it never forgot how to be healthy.

Then there are the other stretches.

The ones where it feels like my skull is splitting open from the inside, and the room tilts, and I am not sure if I am going to throw up, pass out, or both.

Right now, I am somewhere in the middle.

Not great. Not terrible.

Just bearable.

"Please," I say. "I will stay close to the wall."

Mom hesitates, chewing the inside of her cheek. Then she sighs and nods.

"Okay. But I am right here, alright? If you feel weird…"

"I always feel weird," I say, trying to make it a joke. It does not land.

She unclips the wires she can, leaves the ones she cannot, and helps me swing my legs over the side of the bed. The floor is cold against my bare feet. My muscles feel like they have forgotten what they are supposed to do, but they still remember enough to hold my weight when I stand.

"Just a little walk," Mom says. "To the door and back."

I nod, even though I already know I am going farther than that.

We make it to the doorway. My hand drags along the wall as I step into the hallway. The hospital feels smaller out here, the corridor narrowing with machines and carts and quiet voices drifting from other rooms. A nurse at the far end looks up and gives me a polite smile, the kind they reserve for kids who clearly don't want to be here.

For the first few steps, it is okay.

My legs are shaky, but they work.

The headache backs off, dull instead of blinding.

The dizziness is still there, but more like I spun around in a chair one too many times, not like the floor is actively betraying me.

These are the pockets of calm.

The sixty second miracles.

The little lies my body tells me.

I never trust them.

But I still take them.

Because when you have felt awful for months, even a few seconds of almost okay feels like a promise that maybe you are not completely falling apart.

"Slow down," Mom says softly behind me, even though I am barely moving.

We make it halfway down the hall.

That is when it hits.

Pain slams into the back of my skull so fast it steals the air from my lungs. It is sharp and cold and blinding, like someone drove an ice pick straight through my head and twisted. My vision jolts sideways. The overhead lights smear into streaks. The floor tilts under my feet.

I reach for the wall and miss by an inch.

The world lurches.

A sound rips out of me, somewhere between a gasp and a choke.

"Rett?"

Mom's voice goes high and panicked. Hands grab at my arms. My knees buckle, like strings cut from a marionette.

Everything turns into noise.

"Hey, I have got him."

"Careful, careful."

"Let us get him back in the room."

The hallway spins, the ceiling tilting in and out of my vision. My stomach flips so hard I am sure I am going to be sick. My heart hammers against my ribs like it is trying to punch its way out.

"I am fine," I try to say, but it comes out fuzzy, the words slurring together.

I am not fine.

I know I am not fine.

And that scares me way more than the spinning does.

By the time I can focus again, I am back in my bed. A blood pressure cuff squeezes my arm. A pulse ox pinches my finger. Someone is adjusting the head of the bed, raising me up further. Mom stands off to the side, one hand over her mouth, tears running down her face in silent lines.

"BP is a little low."

"Pulse is elevated."

"Any loss of consciousness?"

"He almost went down," Mom says, her voice shaking. "He said he was okay and then he just…"

"We are going to check him over again," a nurse says. Her tone is calm and professional, like this is all just another step in the process. "Rett, can you look at me?"

I blink up at her. Her features blur at the edges, but I manage to lock onto her eyes.

"Headache?" she asks.

"Yes," I whisper.

"Dizziness?"

"Yes."

"Nausea?"

I swallow. "A little."

Her lips press into a line. "Alright. We will page the doctor. Just try to breathe."

Easy for her to say.

My chest feels tight. Not from pain exactly, but from something colder. It spreads through me like ice water, filling up all the space the air is supposed to go.

Clean.

The word keeps echoing in my head.

Clean scans. Clean tests. Nothing wrong.

So why does it feel like something inside me is tearing itself apart?

If everything is clean, then what is doing this to me?

What is getting worse?

What is going to happen next?

Voices blur together on the other side of the curtain.

"Repeat vitals in ten."

"Should we call neuro again?"

"Let us see the labs from this morning."

Then through all the overlapping noise, another voice threads in. Not loud. Not sharp. Not rushed.

Just steady.

"Rett?"

I turn my head toward the doorway.

He is there, the specialist. The guy from before. One hand on the doorframe like he is asking permission to come in without actually saying it. His eyes flick over me, taking in the wires, the cuff, the way my fingers clench the blanket.

He does not move closer.

He does not bark orders.

He does not talk over the nurse or step into the doctor's space.

He just looks at me.

Really looks at me.

"Rett," he repeats, a little softer. "Rough moment, huh?"

My throat is too dry to answer, so I just nod.

The nurse glances at him. "He had a dizzy spell walking in the hall. Almost collapsed."

"I see." He nods once, like he is filing it away somewhere important. "Mind if I stay for a minute? Just to check in?"

He is technically asking the nurse, but his eyes are on me.

It is weird how much that matters.

I manage another small nod.

"Okay," he says simply. "I will hang out in the back. You focus on breathing."

In. Out.
In. Out.

The nurse finishes with the cuff and steps away to chart something. Mom moves closer and wraps her fingers around mine. They are cold. Or maybe mine are. It is hard to tell.

The specialist stays near the wall, out of everyone's way. He does not stare at the monitor, does not rush to flip through my chart. He just keeps me in his line of sight, calm and steady, like he is anchoring the room without touching anything.

And somehow, even though my head is still pounding and the edges of my vision will not quite sharpen, something inside me loosens the tiniest bit.

I don't understand what he does or why he is here.

But right now, in this mess of alarms and questions and people who don't know what is wrong with me, he is the only one who looks at me like I am more than the worst thing happening in my body.

Like I am still a person in the middle of all this.

Someone worth seeing.

And for reasons I cannot explain, that makes the next breath just a little easier to take.

Chapter 6 – The Days Between

They don't release me after the collapse.

At first, the doctors say they want to keep me "overnight, just to be safe," but that turns into two nights, then five, then a week. After the first seven days, they stop giving numbers, which is how I know things are worse than anyone is saying.

Time feels strange here. Days melt together, stretching long and then collapsing in on themselves. I start recognizing the shift change patterns more than the sunrises. I learn the difference between the squeak of the supply cart wheels and the rattle of the meal trays. I memorize voices, footsteps, the click, click, click of the blood pressure cuff inflating around my arm.

Every time a doctor murmurs something like "maybe we can get you home soon," my body decides to prove them wrong.

A dizzy spell when I stand up too fast.

A crushing headache that drops me back onto the pillow.

A spike in my heart rate.

A fainting episode when I try to walk five feet.

Enough to keep me here.

Enough to keep everyone scared.

One afternoon, a nurse walks in quietly while adjusting her badge. She looks young but calm in the way only people who know exactly what they're doing ever look.

"Hi, Rett," she says softly as she checks the IV line. "Just changing this out for a fresh bag."

She works efficiently, moving with smooth confidence, her ponytail swinging as she steps around the bed.

"Let me know if you need anything," she says.

Then she's gone.

I barely have time to process the interaction before another round of vitals begins, then another round of tests. She's just another nurse on the rotation. Nothing more, nothing less.

It's later in the week when he shows up again, the specialist.

He appears in the doorway the same way he did the first time: one shoulder resting lightly against the frame, one hand tucked into his pocket, eyes scanning me like he's checking the weather. Calm. Steady. Patient. He never walks in without making sure he's not interrupting something. He never acts like he owns the room.

"Mind if I come in?" he asks.

It's always a question, never an assumption.

I shrug. "You're already halfway there."

He smiles, not a big ne, just a slight lift at the corner of his mouth, and steps inside.

After that, he starts showing up almost every day.

Sometimes early.

Sometimes late.

Sometimes right when I'm starting to spiral and Mom's hands won't stop shaking.

Then one day, he taps on the door frame.

"You wanna go for a walk? Come on," he says, nodding toward the hallway. "I want to show you something."

"I realized, I don't even know your name." I admit. "You've been visiting me for a couple weeks now, and I haven't asked you."

He laughs, "You can call me Patch. Everyone else here does."

I don't really feel like going anywhere, but something in his voice makes it hard to say no. He walks slow enough that I don't feel rushed. When we turn the corner, I see a wide glass door with a painted sign above it:

The Common Room

He pushes it open, and the smell hits me first, popcorn, faint and warm, like a movie theater that's been shrunk into hospital size.

"All the kids call it, *the Commons*." He tells me.

Inside, it looks nothing like the rest of the building.

There's a TV area, two couches pushed together and a stack of DVDs beside them.

A videogame station sits against one wall with two controllers and a half-finished Mario Kart race frozen on the screen.

There's a puzzle table; pieces scattered everywhere like someone abandoned it mid-thought.

A round table with board games stacked high in the center.

Another with markers and coloring books. A few kids are around—some talking softly, some hooked up to IV poles but laughing anyway, some curled into beanbags watching cartoons.

It doesn't feel like a hospital.

It feels… inviting.
Warm.
Alive.

Patch gestures around like he's presenting some magical kingdom.

"This is where people go when they need a break from being a patient," he says. "You don't need a prescription to hang out here."

I swallow, unsure. "Is it… okay? If I'm here?"

"It's more than okay." He scans the room. "Pick whatever makes your brain hurt the least."

I gravitate toward the board games because they seem less intimidating than the kids who look like they already belong. The man pulls a cart closer, loaded with more games than I've seen in one place.

"You choose," he says, nudging the stack toward me.

I pick Connect 4 because anything with strategy feels like too much. He sits across from me, pretending not to let me win, dropping his last piece in place just when I think I might have him.

"You're messing with me," I mutter.

"Am I?" he asks with fake innocence.

"Yes."

He laughs. A warm, low, grounding laugh. And for a second, the whole room feels lighter.

During our third rematch, the conversation slips somewhere deeper without either of us meaning for it to.

"This sucks," I say quietly, staring at the plastic grid. "Feeling like this. Being stuck here."

He doesn't correct me.

Doesn't panic.

Doesn't throw positivity at me like a bucket of ice water.

He just… waits.

Gives me space.

"It feels like I'm dying," I whisper.

The words hit the air and hover there.

Sharp.
Heavy.
True.

He doesn't look away.

"Feels that big, huh?" he asks gently.

I nod, blinking fast. "Yeah. It does."

He doesn't try to talk me out of it.

Doesn't hand me a platitude.

He just sits in the fear with me. Right there at a board game table with kids laughing two couches over.

"You don't have to pretend its small," he says eventually. "And you don't have to sit in it alone."

My throat is dry, and for a second I think I might fall apart over a children's game. He doesn't rush me. Doesn't fill the silence. He just stays.

And maybe that's why, later that week, when he walks with me into the commons again and points at the video game station, I almost smile.

"You ever played Madden?" he asks.

"All the time." I respond.

"That's perfect. But be warned, I will not take it easy on you." He warns.

He hands me a controller. We fumble through teams and controls, and we split wins 50/50, but who cares when he's narrating each play like a dramatic sports announcer who somehow got trapped inside a children's hospital?

The next time it's Fortnite.

I die instantly.

He tries to revive me.

We both get knocked and eliminated in under two minutes.

For the first time in months, I don't feel sick.

I feel like a kid.

Then the conversations start shifting again. It's slow at first, small pieces at a time. A memory I didn't plan to share slips out. A detail about school. A story about football. An admission that I miss the version of myself who didn't hurt all the time.

He listens like every word matters, like none of it is too small or too dramatic or too much.

And in the quiet moments; when the games are off, when the room is dim, when the fear gets too big to swallow. He stays. He listens. He talks enough to remind me I'm not drifting alone.

Two weeks blur by like that.

Two weeks of tests, of symptoms flaring up whenever freedom feels close.

Two weeks of long nights where Mom sleeps in the chair and Dad pretends he's not crying in the hallway.

Two weeks of nurses popping in to check vitals, always gentle, always quick.

Two weeks of the specialist becoming the one steady part of the day I actually look forward to.

One night, when the pain is a dull roar behind my eyes and the room feels too small to breathe in, something breaks loose inside me.

"What's wrong?" he asks softly, standing in the doorway, waiting to come in. "Everything okay, Rett?"

"It doesn't matter," I mumble, staring at the blanket. "You wouldn't understand."

He doesn't rush to reassure me. He doesn't give me that adult look. The one that tries to smooth everything over with false calm. He just watches me, steady and quiet, like he's deciding whether to step onto fragile ground.

"I do understand," he says finally.

I shake my head, half annoyed, half exhausted. "How? You're not the one stuck here. You're not the one—" My voice cracks. "You don't know what this feels like."

"I'm going to tell you a story." He says. It's not a question.

He steps inside, settling into the chair. His badge catches the soft yellow light.

Patrick Schwartz

"I thought everyone called you Patch?" I ask. "Your badge says Patrick."

"You caught me." He says jokingly. "Let me share my story. It'll make sense to you in a couple of minutes."

I hold up my hands, in surrender and listen to his story.

"When I was your age," he says gently, "my sister, Jessi… she died."

The words land like a punch, not because he says them harshly, but because he says them with the kind of softness you only hear from someone whose wound has scarred but never fully healed.

"She was everything to me," he continues softly. "Bright. Loud. Brave. Cheerleader. She lived bigger than anyone I knew. And then one night, everything changed."

He swallows, the memory bringing a softness to his voice.

"There was a car accident. She wasn't driving." He pauses. "I was. I blamed myself for a long time, trying to figure out how to breathe again while feeling like I didn't deserve to. Our family… we didn't know how to function after that. None of us did. My dad went silent and angry. My mom disappeared into her own pain for a while."

My heart stutters. Something in the way he says it, the rhythm of the details, the shape of the pain, it feels too real, too specific. A story that didn't come from a textbook or a support manual. A story he lived.

"She had these moments," he goes on, voice steady now, thoughtful, "Where she would look right at you and it felt like she saw every version of you at once. The good. The bad. The scared. After she died, I spent a long time trying to be someone she'd still be proud of."

He glances down at his badge.

"And that's why people call me Patch," he adds. "I'm Patrick Schwartz. She used to call me Patch, a nickname I absolutely hated while she was alive." A small, sad smile touches his face. "Now it's how I carry her with me every day."

The room goes still. Almost like the world has paused to let the truth settle. I don't know what to say. I don't know how to hold something that heavy without breaking, especially when I'm already cracked all over.

But somehow, hearing it… hearing him… softens something inside me that's been locked up tight.

He lifts his eyes again, steady and kind.

"So, Rett… when you say I don't get it?" He shakes his head gently. "Trust me. I understand pieces of your fear better than you think."

His words settle into me like a warm weight. Grounding instead of crushing.

For the first time, the fear in my chest doesn't feel like it has to be carried alone.

And for the first time, I trust him completely.

Chapter 7 – Borrowed Strength

The days keep stacking up, blurring together in the way only hospital time can.
Breakfast trays. Vitals. Tests. Symptoms rising and falling like tides.

And then, without warning, December arrives.

I only know because someone taped a paper snowflake to the whiteboard and wrote 12/18 in blue marker. A nurse hums a Christmas song under her breath while checking my IV. The hallways smell faintly like cinnamon from the cafeteria.

It hits me all at once.

Christmas is coming.

My last Christmas.

I don't tell anyone that part.

Not Mom, not Dad, not Patch. But the thought digs in deep, curling under my ribs and holding on.

The Commons changes overnight.

One afternoon I wheel myself in and almost don't recognize it. Paper chains loop across the ceiling. A crooked cardboard tree has been taped to one wall, covered in construction paper ornaments. Someone has draped tinsel over the television. A stack of wrapped gifts sits on a folding table with a hand-lettered sign that says FOR ANYONE.

A boy in a wheelchair is wearing a Santa hat that keeps slipping over his eyes. A little girl with a bald head and a reindeer sweater is helping a nurse tape snowflakes to the windows. Christmas music hums softly from somewhere in the background, not loud enough to hurt my head.

Patch stands near the puzzle table wearing an elf hat that looks like it came from a dollar store clearance bin.

"Don't say a word," he warns when he sees me staring.

I laugh before I can stop myself. It surprises both of us.

We play games that afternoon. Not Madden. Not Fortnite. Stuff that feels smaller and easier. Uno. Candy Land. A goofy snowman stacking game that makes everyone groan when it collapses. For a little while the Commons feels less like a hospital and more like some weird, broken version of a holiday party.

I catch myself watching the other kids.

Some of them are worse than me. Some of them look so tired it scares me. But when Patch makes a terrible joke or someone wins a game, they light up anyway. They laugh anyway.

It makes something twist inside my chest.

If they can smile here, maybe I can too.

A few days later, something strange happens.

I wake up and I don't feel awful.

My head still aches, yeah, but it is dull. Manageable.

The dizziness is quieter. My stomach does not roll when I sit up. I swing my legs over the bed slowly, waiting for the crash, but it does not come.

It feels like a truce.

A tiny, fragile one.

Patch notices first.

"Well, look at you," he says, stepping in with his hands in his pockets. "You are sitting up without looking like the world is sideways."

"I am trying something new," I say.

"What is that?"

I swallow. "Hope."

He gives me a soft smile. The one that means he understands without needing details.

The doctors notice next.

Then the nurses.

Then my parents, who cling to the change like it is a Christmas miracle.

Nobody can explain it.

But I can.

It is Christmas. And I am not spending it here.

Every good moment feels like something I am building on purpose. Like part of me is clawing its way back to the surface through sheer force of will. I want to wake up in my bed. I want to see the tree lights. I want to smell cookies baking and argue with my dad about which movie to watch. I want to take a picture with my mom even if I look pale and exhausted.

I want one last normal holiday before everything falls apart.

I want to go home.

Then one afternoon, the wobble comes back.

It is small at first. Just a sudden pressure behind my eyes. A faint tilt to the room. But my heart slams into my ribs like it remembers every other time this has happened.

I freeze in the middle of the Commons, my hand tightening on the back of a chair.

Not now. Please, not now.

Patch notices immediately.

"Hey," he says softly, stepping closer but not touching me. "Talk to me."

"My head," I whisper. "It feels… wrong."

He watches my face carefully. "Is it spinning or stabbing?"

"Spinning."

"Okay," he says calmly. "Just sit."

I do. Slowly. Carefully. The room wobbles for a long second, then steadies.

Patch crouches in front of me, meeting my eyes.

"You still here?" he asks.

I nod.

"Good," he says. "Just breathe with me for a minute."

In. Out. In. Out.

After a while the pressure eases. The fear does not vanish, but it loosens its grip.

"Thought I was losing it," I murmur.

"Not losing it," he says quietly. "Just scared."

That night, when the Commons is empty and the decorations glow softly in the dim light, I finally say the thing I have been holding back.

"What if this is fake?" I ask. "What if I get worse again as soon as I believe it?"

Patch does not pretend to know the answer.

"Maybe you will," he says gently. "But that does not mean this part isn't real."

I frown. "It does not?"

"No," he says. "It means you are allowed to feel good when good shows up. Even if it is temporary."

"That feels dangerous."

"It is," he admits. "But it is also human."

By the end of the week, the improvement is impossible to ignore. The doctors start talking discharge again, cautiously, carefully, like they are afraid the universe might hear them and change its mind.

Patch stops by that night, and the room settles into a comfortable silence. The kind you only share with someone you trust. After a moment, something nudges at the back of my mind, and before I can stop myself, I ask:

"Do you have somewhere to be on Christmas? I mean, I don't know how this job works. I just… didn't know if you would be here."

His eyebrows lift, surprised. A friendly grin pulls at his mouth.

"That is kind of you to ask," he says. "But yes. I have a family to get home to."

"Oh." I don't know why I feel disappointed.

"My wife actually works here," he adds. "Aliza. She is a nurse here. You have met her, even if you don't realize it."

My mind flashes to the ponytail, the calm voice, the badge.

"And my daughter," he continues, "her name is Jessi. She is little. Full of energy."

"Jessi," I say softly.

He nods.

"I just didn't want you to spend it alone," I admit.

"I will not," he says. "And neither will you."

Something loosens in my chest.

"Wanting something that badly," he says, "sometimes it is enough to give you a little borrowed strength."

I swallow.

Because I know what I am borrowing from.

The next morning the doctor comes in smiling.

"If things stay stable," he says, "I think we can get you home before Christmas."

Mom cries. Dad exhales. Patch catches my eye from the hall. And for the first time in a long time, hope feels real enough to touch.

Chapter 8 – The Gift of Presence

The thing nobody ever warns you about being sick is how good, *good* feels.

Like, not just better, not “less dizzy” or “less nauseous”, but actually good.

It’s been three days since I left the hospital, and every morning I wake up afraid the calm will break. That the aching pulse in my skull will come roaring back. That I’ll stand up and the room will tilt sideways.

But it hasn’t.

Not once.

And today, Christmas Eve, I feel lighter than I have in months.

Mom insists on checking my forehead twice before I even get out of bed, and Dad keeps clearing his throat like he’s trying to ask if I’m okay without sounding like he’s hovering. But the truth is: I’m more than okay. I’m clear. I’m steady. I’m… me.

We’re heading out to run a few last-minute errands. “Just stocking stuffers,” Mom promises; but as soon as we walk into the first store, I know exactly what I want to do.

“I need to get something,” I tell them.

Dad raises an eyebrow. “Something specific?”

“Something for you guys.”

Mom’s face softens instantly. “Rett, honey, you don’t have to…”

“I want to,” I cut in gently. “Really.”

They exchange one of those parent glances. The kind that's half worried, half proud. Then Mom hands me a twenty, Dad hands me another, and I pretend I don’t see Dad slip an extra five in my coat pocket “just in case.”

Once they wander off to “accidentally” give me space, I walk the aisles slower than usual. Not because I’m scared to collapse, because I want to take it all in. The lights strung across the ceiling. The rush of shoppers in coats dusted with snow. Kids tugging their parents toward toy displays. Carols drifting from cheap speakers overhead.

It feels like life humming, warm and vibrant and alive.

I end up buying Mom a small silver necklace with a tiny snowflake charm. She’s always loved snow. Says it feels magical, like the world is quieting down just for her. When I see it hanging in the glass case, it already feels like hers.

For Dad, I find a thick pair of Bengals socks. They are bright orange with the logo right near the ankle. They’re ridiculous and loud and exactly the type of thing he’d pretend to hate and then wear every single day.

I carry the bag out of the store like its precious.

Because it is.

Because giving feels good.

Because *being here* feels even better.

That evening, we drive to Grandma and Grandpa's house for the yearly Christmas Eve party. The second we step inside; warmth hits me from every angle. Loud voices overlapping, kids running through hallways, the smell of ham and cinnamon rolls mingling in the air.

Aunt Julie hugs me tight enough to crack a rib. Grandpa pats my shoulder like he's checking whether I'm real. My cousins swarm me, peppering me with questions.

"You feeling good?"
"You back for good?"
"You look taller! Did the hospital stretch you?"

I laugh at all of it.

We sit down to dinner. It's a feast that looks like

Thanksgiving had a baby with a Christmas card.

Afterward, we gather in the living room for a white elephant.

Someone brings a pair of giant fuzzy slippers shaped like bear paws. Someone else contributes a peanut brittle tin that may or may not be from last year. I end up with a fishing hat covered in lights that blink whenever you tap the brim.

It's chaotic in the best way.

Later, the adults hand out matching pajamas. Red flannel with Christmas trees on them. Mine are too big, and Mom blames the store for "inconsistent sizing," but I know the truth. She wasn't buying pajamas. She was buying the possibility of more time.

I don't say anything.

I just put them on and smile.

We all cram into the basement to watch *National Lampoon's Christmas Vacation*, because Grandpa says it "builds character." He laughs so hard at the squirrel scene he wheezes until Grandma whacks him with a dish towel.

I laugh, too. Big, full belly laughs that shake the dust loose in my chest. I can't remember the last time laughing didn't hurt. Tonight, it feels effortless.

After the movie, Mom reads a short Christmas story from a tattered book she's had since she was a kid. I've heard it a hundred times, but tonight it lands deeper. Softer. Like it's folding itself somewhere safe inside me.

When it's time to head home, I'm exhausted, but not the sick kind of exhausted. Just regular, normal, holiday tired. The kind you get from being happy and warm and full.

Back home, we follow our last tradition: opening **one present** on Christmas Eve.

I tear the paper slowly, savoring it, and inside is a soft gray hoodie, it's simple, comfortable, exactly my style.

"It reminded me of you," Dad says.

"It's perfect," I tell him. And I mean it.

After my parents head upstairs, I linger in the living room, letting the glow from the tree wash over me. Twinkling lights reflect off the ornaments. Little blurs of red, green, and gold. The room is warm and silent, the kind of peaceful that feels almost sacred.

I curl my legs under me on the couch and pull the hoodie tighter around my torso.

For a moment, I close my eyes.

If this is my last Christmas… it's a good one.

The thought doesn't hurt.

It just settles. Soft. Gentle. Real.

I breathe in the pine scent of the tree and exhale slow.

I'm here.

I'm alive.

I'm home.

Tomorrow is Christmas.

And for once in what seems like forever, I can't wait.

I'm actually excited.

Chapter 9 – The Christmas We Needed

I wake to the soft glow of the Christmas tree lights flickering through the crack beneath my bedroom door.

For a moment, I just lie there, listening to the stillness of the house. No pounding headache. No dizziness. No tightness in my chest.

Just quiet.

I sit up slowly, half expecting the world to tilt sideways, but it doesn't.

For a second, I just stare at my hands, confused.

I feel good, like actually good. For the first time in months, there is no pain, light or intense, pounding from within my head.

And it's not a fluke.

Ever since they discharged me from the hospital, the headaches, the dizziness, the nausea, *the waves*… they've all been quiet. Like someone finally hit pause on whatever's been tearing me apart.

I breathe in once, slow and steady, shocked and even grateful. I push myself to my feet. My legs don't wobble. My vision doesn't smear. I move down the hallway and into the living room, half afraid this moment will shatter if I blink too hard.

Mom is standing near the tree in her fuzzy red pajamas, a mug of cocoa warming her hands. Her hair is pulled up in a messy bun that only appears on holidays and late nights. The second she sees me upright and steady; her whole face softens.

"Hey, sweetheart," she says. "Merry Christmas."

Dad pokes his head out from the kitchen, spatula in hand. "Well, look at that. Up before noon. Christmas miracle!"

I roll my eyes, but warmth nudges at my ribs.

Because for once… they aren't hovering. They aren't whispering behind closed doors. They aren't scared.

Not today.

I settle cross legged on the carpet the way I used to when I was little, and Mom hands me the first present. It's a snowman wrapped package with tape lines so crooked it has to be hers.

Inside is a new white tiger Cincinnati Bengals Jersey. Centered on the back, a single number 1, with Chase written above it. I pull it over my head immediately and begin jumping around the living room.

"We thought you might like this," Dad says. "You know. For game days."

I laugh, looking at myself in the reflection of the entry way mirror. "Thanks. I love it."

Next, Mom gives me a small, tightly wrapped box. Inside is a brand-new controller for my Xbox.

"You dropped yours when you passed out a while ago," she says quietly.

My breath catches, but instead of spiraling, I reach forward and hug her. "Thank you," I whisper.

When I pull away, she wipes quickly under her eyes, pretending she's not emotional. Dad pretends not to notice.

The room smells like pine and cinnamon. Wrapping paper piles around my feet. Stockings overflow. For a few minutes, I'm not a kid who lives in hospitals or worries about collapsing in hallways. I'm just a fifteen-year-old opening presents on Christmas morning.

And it feels like magic.

Breakfast tastes like a holiday should. We have scrambled eggs, cinnamon rolls, bacon, and fruit. Warmth fills my chest as I eat more than I've managed in weeks.

Dad raises his coffee mug. "To feeling better."

Mom lifts hers too, eyes shining.

I hesitate, then clink glasses with them. It feels like calling something true into existence.

But every now and then, a shadow edges its way in.

This might be the last time.

My last Christmas morning.

My last presents.

My last everything.

I shove the thought down each time.

Today isn't about fear.

Today is about being alive.

Grandma arrives at four with two casseroles she warns are "experimental." Dad carves a ham that looks big enough to feed the entire neighborhood. Mashed potatoes spill over the rim of the bowl. Corn, green beans, rolls, and gravy. The food fills the whole table.

I pile my plate high.

People laugh and talk over each other. Grandma pats my shoulder every few minutes, saying I look "rosy." Mom smooths my hair back like she did when I was little. Dad tells the same joke about the ham being "undercooked" despite checking the temperature three separate times.

I hold onto every sound, every smell, every smile.

I memorize it.

After dinner, we play games. From Uno to Sequence to Scrabble. Mom insists on winning all of them. Dad insists she only wins because of luck and not skill. Grandma invents questionable Scrabble words that spark a ten-minute argument.

I don't care what game we're playing.

I just love hearing everyone laugh.

For the first time in what feels like forever, I lean back in my chair and close my eyes without fear that the world will start tipping sideways. Their voices swirl around me.

Comforting, alive, real.

It hits me how much I've missed this.

How much I needed this.

We end the night with a Christmas movie. Dad picks *Elf*, probably because I know he's watched *Christmas Vacation* at least three times this week.

I curl onto the couch under a blanket. Mom rests her head on my shoulder. Dad sits at the end and taps my foot with his, checking, quietly, that I'm still okay.

The glow from the tree lights flickers across the room. The movie plays. I laugh, real laughter that doesn't make my head throb.

I echo my favorite line, "*You sit on a throne of lies.*"

For two hours, I forget what it feels like to be sick.

When the credits roll, I stay still for a long moment. The room is warm and quiet except for Mom's soft snore. Dad pretends he isn't asleep.

And the thought gently settles inside me:

If this is my last Christmas…

I'm okay with that.

Because today was perfect.

It doesn't hurt.

It doesn't crush me.

It simply… is.

I pull the blanket tighter and breathe in the pine scent from the tree.

Today, I wasn't sick.

Today, I wasn't scared.

Today, I was just me.

And I'll hold onto that.

No matter what comes next.

Chapter 10 – Almost Normal

The night before school starts again, something shifts.

Not physically. Just… in the air around me.

A quiet spark.

A pull toward normal life that I haven't felt in a long time.

I set my backpack on the bed and start getting ready like this is any other Sunday night.

Notebooks in.

Folders organized.

Pencils sharpened.

My water bottle washed and ready.

Then I lay out my clothes for the morning; jeans, my new grey hoodie, my clean sneakers. The simple routine feels good. Familiar. Almost comforting.

Mom pauses in my doorway on her way down the hall. She takes in the neatly folded outfit, the packed bag, the way I'm actually moving with some energy.

"You're all set for tomorrow?" she asks, careful not to sound too eager.

"Yeah," I say, trying to play it cool. "Feels weird, but… good."

She nods, a soft smile tugging at her mouth. There's something fragile in her eyes, like she's scared to believe this could last.

When I finally climb under the covers, it's the first time in a long while that the next day doesn't feel like something to survive.

It feels like something to return to.

Sleep comes easier than I expect.

The first day back feels bright and honestly kind of exciting.

Mom drives me to school with the radio low, doing her best not to stare holes through me. She watches me the way you watch a glass ornament you're afraid will drop but don't want to hover over too closely.

"You look rested," she says.

"I kind of am," I admit.

Walking through the school doors feels surreal in a good way.

Lockers slam.

Kids shout across hallways.

The building hums with energy I didn't realize I missed.

A few people wave or call my name.

"Hey! You're back!"

"Rett! Dude!"

"You feeling better?"

And for once, I don't shrink under the attention.

I smile.

It feels easy.

In second period, a friend from PE makes a joke about how he thought I'd transferred to Antarctica, and I laugh harder than I intend to. It feels natural, like a reflex I haven't used in a while but didn't forget.

Throughout the week, everything stays… steady.

Not perfect.

Just steady.

A little headache here.

A dizzy flicker one afternoon.

A moment where the classroom lights feel too bright.

But nothing that stops me.

Nothing that knocks me backward.

I tell myself this is what getting better looks like, tiny steps, quiet progress, and a slow climb back into my life.

Then the ground gives out beneath me.

It's the next Monday, right between third and fourth period. The hallway is chaos. Students weaving in every direction, lockers clanging, teachers holding half-finished coffee cups.

I'm walking with a couple friends from PE, still laughing about a dodgeball comeback I swear didn't actually violate the rules, when something inside me slips.

At first, it's so small I almost miss it. It's just a strange weight behind my eyes and a quick flutter in my vision.

Then the flutter becomes a pulse.

A sharp, heavy heartbeat; too loud, too close.

The lights overhead blur.

The hallway tilts, just slightly, but enough to throw me off balance.

"Rett? You okay?" someone asks.

I blink.

Try to focus.

Try to breathe normally.

The air suddenly feels thick.

My legs go weak.

Voices stretch and warp.

Colors smear together.

I reach out for a locker to steady myself, but my fingers skim the metal and miss completely.

And then everything falls away.

My knees crash into the floor.

The world pitches sideways.

Someone shouts my name.

It sounds far away, and it's fading fast.

I hit the tile hard.

Cold.

Unforgiving.

The noise around me dulls into a low hum, the kind you hear underwater.

The ceiling blurs.

Then disappears.

Chapter 11 – The Wrong Kind of Nothing

Sirens come in pieces.

First the feeling, this low, distant vibration under my ribs. Then the sound, thin and far away, getting louder and louder until it drills through the fog in my head.

Something rough presses against the back of my skull. The air smells like plastic and metal and something sharp I can't name.

"…Rett? Can you hear me?"

I try to open my eyes.

Light explodes.

I squeeze them shut again with a groan.

"Alright, bud," a voice says, steady but tight, right above me. "You passed out at school. You're in the ambulance. Just keep breathing for me, okay?"

Ambulance.

The word hits like a punch.

I remember the hallway. The jokes. The locker I tried to grab and missed. The tile rushing up. Then nothing.

I force my eyes open again, slower this time.

The ceiling is white and close. There's a strip of lights that looks like it's buzzing even if it isn't. A paramedic leans over me, his face lined and serious. There's something strapped across my chest. A cuff squeezes my arm, then let's go.

"How's your head?" he asks.

"Bad," I rasp.

"Dizzy?"

"Yes."

"Nausea?"

"Yeah."

The questions feel familiar. Too familiar. Like I've somehow signed up for the worst loyalty program ever.

The back doors rattle. The ambulance sways. My stomach flips, but I'm not sure if it's from the motion or the fear clawing its way up my throat.

This wasn't supposed to happen.

I did everything right. I went back to school. I took it slow. I listened when Mom hovered and let Dad pretend, he wasn't watching me like a hawk.

I was getting better.

I was.

So why am I here again?

The siren wails louder, then shifts in pitch as we turn. The paramedic's voice blurs for a second. I close my eyes and count my breaths.

In.

Out.

In.

Out.

It doesn't help.

All I can think is one thing:

What if this is it?

Again.

The ER is chaos in slow motion.

Fluorescent lights. Curtains on tracks. Voices layered over each other: orders, questions, phones ringing, someone crying a few bays away.

I'm lying on a different bed now. The gurney? A stretcher? I've lost track of the vocabulary of being horizontal.

My clothes feel wrong. My hoodie is gone. There's a thin hospital gown I don't remember putting on. Electrodes cling to my chest like cold stickers.

Mom appears first, breathless, cheeks flushed, hair frizzing out of her bun.

"Rett." She's at my side in three strides, her hand on my face, then my arm, then my hair, like she can't decide which part of me she needs to confirm is still here.

"Oh my gosh. Oh my gosh. Are you okay? They called from the school and said…"

"I'm fine," I lie automatically.

I am absolutely not fine.

Tears spill over anyway. Hers, not mine. Mine are still stuck somewhere behind my ribs.

Dad comes in a beat later, moving slower, like he's holding something in by pure force.

"Hey, champ," he says, voice too calm. "Heard you decided to take a nap in the hallway."

It's a joke. I know it's a joke.

Another joke that doesn't land.

A nurse steps in with a blood pressure cuff and a tablet. "We're going to keep monitoring him," she says. "The doctor's reviewing his history."

His history.

Like I'm a file. A chart. A list of tests that all say the same thing.

Nothing.

Hours blur.

They run bloodwork again.

They hook me up to an IV "just to keep you hydrated."

They wheel me through the same big tube for another MRI. The machine thumps and whirs around my head as I stare at the inside of the tunnel and try not to think about tumors eating my brain.

When it's over, they slide me back into the room and park my bed like a car in a narrow garage.

Mom sits in the chair by the curtain, hands woven so tight together her knuckles are white. Dad paces in a small rectangle near the door.

Nobody says it.

But we're all thinking the same thing:

If something's growing in there, they'll see it now.

If they don't…

I don't know which answer is worse anymore.

The doctor comes in with a tablet tucked under his arm and his expression set in that professional neutral I've learned to hate.

"Rett," he says. "Good to see you again."

I don't bother pretending I'm happy to see him.

He pulls the curtain mostly closed, glances at the monitors, then at my parents. "I've looked over your tests," he says. "The MRI from today compared to the last one, your bloodwork, and your vitals from the ambulance."

Mom leans forward, bracing.

Dad crosses his arms, jaw clenched.

"And?" Mom prompts, voice already shaking.

The doctor exhales through his nose. "Everything looks… normal," he says carefully. "There are no signs of a mass, bleeding, infections, or structural problems in the brain. Your scans are unchanged. Your labs are within expected ranges."

Normal.

Unchanged.

Expected.

The words clang around in my skull like dropped metal.

"So, you're telling me *nothing* is wrong?" Mom's voice jumps an octave. "You saw what happened. He collapsed in the middle of the school hallway…again. He's been having headaches for months, dizzy spells, nausea, fainting. That's not nothing."

"I didn't say nothing," the doctor replies, keeping his tone even. "I said nothing *structural* or *life-threatening* is showing up on our tests right now."

"That's impossible," I blurt, my own voice sounding too loud in my ears. "You're missing something. You have to be."

He looks at me, and for a second his expression softens. "I hear that you're scared," he says. "This is frightening, and I don't want you to think we're ignoring that. Your symptoms are real."

Then he hesitates.

Here it comes.

The part I hate.

"Sometimes," he continues, "when all the physical and neurological tests come back normal, we start to think about how the brain and body work together in other ways. Stress, anxiety, and certain patterns in the nervous system can create very real symptoms; dizziness, fainting, headaches, even weakness and without there being a tumor, or an infection, or something we can see on a scan."

Dad exhales, rubbing a hand over his face. "So… if the tests are clear," he says slowly, "then what *is* causing all of this?"

Mom leans forward slightly. "Are you saying something is happening that we just can't see yet? Or that the tests aren't picking it up?"
Her voice isn't sharp, it just seems tired. Worried.

The doctor hesitates. "What I'm saying is that the symptoms are real. But the cause might not be something structural, which means it may not show up on scans."

Dad frowns. "Then… what does that even mean? His body is just… reacting on its own?"

The room goes still.

And my stomach twists.

Because that's what I heard too.

You're not sick.
You're just you.
Broken.
Wrong.
Too weak to handle stress like a normal person.

"I'm not making this up," I say, heat flooding my cheeks. "I'm not faking. I don't want this."

"I know you don't," the doctor says gently. "Nobody is saying you're faking. Nobody chooses these kinds of symptoms."

He looks between my parents again. "Here's our next step. I want our pediatric neurologist to review everything once more. And I'd also like to refer you to a psychologist who specializes in cases like these; teens with fainting, dizziness, or chronic pain that doesn't show up on scans. She works with how the nervous system processes stress and signals."

Mom swallows. "A… psychologist?"

The word lands with confusion, not rejection.

"It doesn't mean it's all in his head," he reassures her. "The nervous system can get stuck in a fight, or, flight loop. The brain keeps sending danger signals even when there's no actual threat. And the body responds to those signals—sometimes intensely."

"That still doesn't make sense," I say. "I didn't decide to pass out in the hallway."

"Exactly," he says. "You didn't choose any of this. Just like someone doesn't choose a panic attack, or a migraine, or a seizure. The brain can trigger real physical reactions without permission."

He steps closer to the bed. "Your tests are reassuring," he says. "Your symptoms are not. We're not done searching. We just need to start looking at the whole picture."

He turns to my parents. "For now, I'd like to keep him overnight for monitoring. If everything stays stable, we'll discharge him tomorrow with follow-up appointments. Neurology. Psychology. And we'll work together from there."

He waits like he expects one of us to agree.

Nobody does.

When he finally leaves, the curtain swishes shut behind him with a soft hiss that sounds a lot like a period at the end of a sentence I hate.

Silence settles over us like a heavy blanket.

Mom stares at the floor.

Dad stares at the monitor.

I stare at my hands.

"So that's it?" I say eventually, my voice thin and sharp at the edges. "They're just… done? 'Congrats, kid, your brain is wrong, enjoy your fainting spells'?"

"Everett," Mom starts.

"No." The word rips out of me, louder than I mean, too loud for how small I suddenly feel. "I'm serious. They keep saying everything is normal. They keep saying nothing is wrong. Then why do I feel like this? Why do I keep waking up on floors and in ambulances and in hospital beds hooked up to machines if I'm so freaking *normal*?"

My voice breaks completely.

The silence afterward is brutal.

I look away, jaw trembling, hot tears blurring everything. I don't want them to see me cry. I'm so tired of crying.

Mom stands immediately, like something inside her snaps in half, and crosses to my side. She cups the back of my head with shaking hands, threading her fingers through my hair like she's trying to hold what's left of me together.

"Baby…" Her voice is a whisper soaked in fear. "Nobody thinks you're making this up. We know you're hurting. We know you're scared. We see you. We see all of it."

"Do you?" The words slip out before I can stop them, small, cracked, honest. "Because it feels like everyone thinks I'm… broken. Or dramatic. Or…my voice catches."

I swallow deep and focus on the last word. "—crazy."

Mom gasps like I've stabbed her straight through the heart. "Rett, no. Absolutely not. You are not crazy. Not even close."

Dad has been silent for so long I almost forgot he was there. When he finally speaks, his voice is rough, like sandpaper dragged across something that used to be strong.

"We're going to figure this out," he says, and his eyes shine in a way that scares me more than anything the doctors said. "I don't care who we have to see. Neurologists. Psychologists. Specialists in whatever this is. A whole team of them. All of them. I don't care if we have to fly across the country. Someone…*someone* is going to help you. I swear it."

His voice cracks on the last word.

It should comfort me.

It should make me feel safe.

But all I can hear are the doctor's words echoing in a loop I can't shut off:

Nothing dangerous.

Nothing structural.

Nothing wrong.

Nothing.
Nothing.
Nothing.

The wrong kind of nothing…the kind that makes you wonder if the problem isn't in your body at all…

…but in you.

I don't know how long I lie there after they step out to "grab some air." Ten minutes. Thirty. Time is slippery in hospitals.

The curtain rustles again.

For a second, my frustration grows

Just waiting for another doctor with another explanation that doesn't explain anything.

Instead, a familiar voice slips through.

"Hey," Patch says quietly. "Mind if I come in?"

I exhale a breath I didn't realize I was holding. "Pretty sure no one listens when I say no," I mutter.

He steps in anyway, letting the curtain fall halfway closed. No chart in his hands. No tablet. Just him in his polo and badge, hands in his pockets.

"Rough day," he says.

It's not a question.

I stare at the ceiling. "How'd you guess?"

He doesn't take the chair right away. He just stands there for a beat, giving me space like he's waiting to see if I'll shut down or crack open.

"I heard about what the doctor said," he says eventually. "About the tests. The referrals."

"So, you know they think I'm crazy too," I say flatly.

He doesn't flinch.

"I know they think your brain and your body are stuck in some kind of loop," he says. "And that they're trying to figure out how to break it."

I snort. "Cool. So, I'm a glitch."

Patch moves closer and finally sinks into the chair. "Can I tell you something? Not as a specialist or whatever my badge says I am. Just as a guy whose brain has played dirty tricks on him before."

I shrug. "You're going to anyway."

He smiles softly. "When my sister died," he says, "there were months where I was sure my chest was going to explode every time I walked past her room, or heard sirens, or walked through the hallways of my school. I'd get dizzy in grocery stores. My heart would race for no reason. My hands would shake. I couldn't breathe. I had recurring nightmares. I thought I was dying. Again, and again."

I glance over at him.

"You know what all my tests said?" he continues. "Heart? Fine. Lungs? Fine. Blood? Fine. Brain scans? Clean. Perfect. Normal."

The word tastes different coming from him.

"Turns out," he says, "my brain was acting like danger was everywhere, all the time. It was trying to protect me from something that had already happened by seeing danger in things that weren't dangerous anymore."

"That sounds stupid," I say, but my voice is quieter now.

"It felt stupid," he agrees. "But the reactions were real. The sweat. The shaking. The racing heart. The dizziness. My body wasn't lying. It was just… overreacting."

He leans back a little. "Sometimes," he says, "when doctors can't find a physical 'thing'. Like a tumor, a bleed, or a broken bone. They start looking at how the nervous system is firing. Not because they think you're making it up. But because they believe you *so much* that they need a different way to explain what's happening."

I stare at the blanket, fist gripping the fabric, knuckles turning white. "What if I don't want that explanation?" I whisper. "What if I need this to be something they can cut out or fix or… or point at on a scan and say, 'There it is, we got it'?"

Patch is quiet for a long moment.

"I get that," he says finally. "A visible enemy is easier than an invisible one. It feels more… legitimate. Less like it's your fault." He pauses. "But I'm going to say this again so you hear it clearly: this isn't your fault."

My eyes begin to water.

I don't know why that's the line that almost breaks me.

"I'm scared," I admit, the words scraping on the way out. "I keep thinking… what if they're wrong? What if there *is* something there and they just can't see it yet? What if this is the beginning of the end and everyone's acting like I'm fine?"

Patch nods slowly. "That 'what if' can eat you alive," he says. "Believe me, I know. But here's the weird thing: whether this is something they can see or something they can't, the way through is the same."

"What do you mean?" I ask.

"You still have to show up," he says. "To appointments. To school. To your own life. You still have to learn how to live with fear sitting in the corner without letting it drive the car. You still have to decide, over and over, that you're more than what's happening in your body."

He gives a half, smile. "And you still have every right to be mad about it."

I let out a shaky breath. "They want me to see a psychologist," I say. "Like, a therapist. For my brain. For my… loop."

He nods. "That sounds like a good idea."

"It makes me feel broken," I mutter.

"You feel broken because you've been through something really hard," he says. "Seeing someone who understands how brains and bodies team up to wreck our lives sometimes? That doesn't make you broken. It means you're willing to fight for yourself."

The word *fight* sits differently than *cope* or *accept.*

It feels less like surrender and more like action.

"I don't know if I can do this," I whisper.

"You don't have to do all of it right now," he says. "You just have to do the next thing."

"What's the next thing?" I ask.

He shrugs. "Tonight? Let them hook you to the monitors. Let yourself be mad. Let yourself be scared. And maybe… let yourself not Google 'brain tumor survival rates' for once."

My cheeks flush hot.

He smiles knowingly. "You're not the first kid to do it," he says. "You won't be the last."

I huff out a breath that's almost a laugh.

Almost.

Patch stands, smoothing his hands on his pants. "I'll be around tomorrow," he says. "We can talk more. Or we can play Madden and you can lose again. Your choice."

"Trash talk from a guy in khakis is wild," I murmur.

"Khakis are powerful," he replies gravely. "Don't underestimate them."

He takes a step toward the curtain, then pauses. "Rett?"

"Yeah?"

"Whatever name they eventually put on this—tumor, no tumor, loop, syndrome, whatever—you're still you," he says. "That doesn't change."

He lets that hang in the air for a second, like a small, solid thing I can pick up if I want to.

Then he slips out of the room.

The curtain sways behind him.

I stare at the ceiling again, listening to the monitor beep steadily beside me.

The fear is still there.

The anger too.

The "what if I'm right?" hasn't gone anywhere.

But there's something else there now, small and stubborn and annoying:

The idea that maybe, just maybe, "nothing" doesn't mean *nothing.*

It just means the fight is going to look different than I expected.

I don't know if I'm ready for that.

But the monitor keeps beeping.

Beep.

Beep.

Beep.

And for now, that has to be enough.

Chapter 12 – A Name for Nothing

I don't sleep much that night.

The monitor hums beside me, its green line drifting in spikes, in rhythm, the numbers steady and unbothered. My body lies still enough to convince a nurse I'm resting, but my mind refuses to join in. It keeps pacing circles in the dark, tight, anxious loops that never quite settle, while the rest of me just… waits.

Nurses come and go, slipping in and out like ghosts.

"Just checking your vitals," one whispers around midnight, as if the beeping isn't already announcing I'm alive.

Blood pressure cuff. Pulse ox. Temperature.

Normal, normal, normal.

I close my eyes and try to sync my breathing with the soft hiss of the oxygen, even though I don't technically need it anymore.

In, out. In, out.

The same rhythm as the monitor, like maybe if I match it, my thoughts will finally quiet.

They don't.

Every time I start to drift, I see the hallway again. The lockers. The floor rising to meet my face. Then sirens. Then the inside of that MRI tunnel. Then the doctor's mouth saying words like *reassuring* and *nothing dangerous* while my whole life feels like it's being shoved toward the edge of a cliff.

At some point, Mom and Dad come back.

I feel Mom's hand in my hair first, gentle, rhythmic strokes like when I was little and had a fever. I keep my eyes closed, pretending to be asleep, because I don't know how to look at her without seeing the way she flinched when I said "crazy."

Dad's voice is a low rumble near the window.

"I don't like it," he murmurs. "A psychologist? Really? He passes out in the middle of school and they want to talk about his feelings?"

"It's not just feelings," Mom whispers back. Her voice is frayed, but not sharp. "You heard what the doctor said. It's his nervous system. His brain… reacting. If this is the path to answers, we can't ignore it."

"So that's it?" Dad sighs. "We're just accepting that it's stress? Anxiety? Whatever buzzword they're using this year?"

There's a long pause.

"It's not about what we're accepting," Mom says quietly. "It's about what we have left. We've ruled out tumors. Bleeds. Infections. Every test comes back clean. If this specialist can help us understand what *is* happening, then we owe it to him to try. I don't want him to feel like… like what he's going through doesn't count unless there's a picture on a scan."

The words punch through my chest.

I swallow hard and keep my eyes shut tighter.

"I know that," Dad says after a moment. "I just… I wanted it to be something we could fix. Something with a surgery or a pill or… *something.*"

His voice shakes. Unsteady.

Mom doesn't answer. The only sound is the monitor and the soft scrape of her thumb across my forehead, over and over, like she's trying to erase the worry lines that weren't there a few months ago.

It's a long time before I finally crash for real, dropping into a sleep that feels more like falling than resting.

Morning comes in pieces.

First the light, seeping in around the edges of the blinds.

Then the sounds. The carts rolling in the hallway, a baby crying somewhere down the corridor, a nurse laughing too loudly at something on her phone.

Then pain, slow and dull behind my eyes. Not as sharp as before, but still there, like a bruise that doesn't know how to fade.

"Good morning, sunshine," a voice says.

I blink my eyes open to find a nurse standing by my bed with a plastic tray. The smell of hospital eggs hits me before I even see the food.

"Morning," I croak.

"How's the head?" she asks, checking the monitor.

"Like it ran into a wall," I say. "But… softer than yesterday."

"Progress," she says, like that's something we can grade.

She adjusts a few things, asks the usual questions, and then leaves me with scrambled eggs, cold toast, and orange juice from concentrate. I pick at all of it without really eating.

Mom is curled up in the chair by the window, wrapped in a hospital blanket. Her hair is a mess. Her eyes are swollen. She still somehow looks like Mom.

Dad is gone.

"Did he leave?" I ask.

She sits up, blinking like she forgot she was in a hospital. "Your dad? He ran home to shower and grab a few things," she says. "He'll be back in a little bit. He didn't want you to wake up alone."

Too late.

I push the eggs around the plate. "Do we… know what's happening yet?"

She exhales slowly. "Not yet. The neurologist is going to look over everything again this morning. And the psychologist that the doctor mentioned—she's supposed to come by and see you today. Just to talk. No tests or anything scary."

My stomach flips anyway.

"Great," I mutter. "Can't wait to unpack my trauma for a stranger."

"Rett," Mom says gently.

"I know," I say, stabbing the toast. "I know. I'm just… tired of being the mystery case."

She doesn't argue.

She just reaches over and hooks her pinky around mine on the bedrail, like she used to do when I was little and getting shots. I stare at our hands and try to pretend I'm not grateful for it.

Dad comes back around nine, smelling like soap and cold air. He has my hoodie and a pair of sweatpants folded over one arm, my phone charger in his hand.

"Brought reinforcements," he says, setting everything on the chair.

"Finally," I say. "I was about to start bartering organs for a working outlet."

He snorts. "Pretty sure that's frowned upon here."

The joke lands better this time.

For a few minutes, things almost feel normal. He untangles the charger while Mom fusses with my pillow. We talk about nothing. Dad mentions some game on TV, a neighbor who put their Christmas lights up too early, the fact that hospital orange juice might actually be a war crime.

For a few minutes, it's just us.

Then there's a knock at the door.

A woman steps in. She's in her forties, maybe, with dark hair pulled into a low ponytail and a blazer that looks too professional for the pediatric wing. She doesn't have a stethoscope, just a clipboard and a small badge that says:

Dr. Lorena Morales, Pediatric Psychology.

"Hi," she says, voice calm but not fake. "Rett?"

"That's me," I say, trying not to shrink into the pillow.

"It's nice to meet you," she says. "I've talked with your medical team and your parents, but I wanted to hear from you too. Mind if I sit?"

I shrug. "Everyone else does."

She smiles a little and pulls the visitor chair closer to the bed.

Mom shifts awkwardly. "Do you… want us to stay?" she asks me.

I think about their conversation last night in the dark. About Dad's voice breaking when he said he wanted something they could fix. About Mom arguing that my pain counts even if it doesn't show up on a screen.

"I don't know," I admit.

Dr. Morales jumps in. "We can start with all of you here," she offers. "If, at any point, you'd rather talk alone, we can do that too. There's no right or wrong way to do this."

I nod, because that feels like the safest option.

She glances at my wristband, then back at me. "So, Rett," she says. "Can you tell me, in your own words, what's been going on?"

The question is so simple it almost makes me laugh.

Instead, I take a breath.

"I get headaches," I say. "Bad ones. And I get dizzy. And sometimes it feels like the floor moves even when it doesn't. Then I pass out. I wake up in places I don't remember getting to.

Ambulances.

Hospital rooms.

There are tests. There's… nothing. Then it happens again."

She nods, not writing anything down yet. Just listening.

"How long has this been happening?" she asks.

"Months," I say. "Since… before school started. It's been progressively getting worse though."

She looks at me for a second like she can see past what I said to all the things I didn't.

"And what's the scariest part of it for you?" she asks.

I stare at the blanket.

"That nobody believes me," I blurt, before I can soften it. "That everyone thinks I'm making it up or exaggerating or just… too anxious or something. Or that it's all in my head. And also, that I'm going to die," I add, because it feels stupid to leave that out. "I keep thinking there's a tumor or something they're missing. That one day I'm not going to wake up."

The room is quiet.

Mom sniffles softly. Dad's hand tightens around the bedrail.

Dr. Morales finally picks up her pen.

"Thank you for being honest," she says. "Those are really understandable fears. I want to be clear about something from the beginning: when doctors like me get involved, it's not because people think you're lying. It's because your symptoms are real, your tests are real, and we need a different kind of science to explain why they're not lining up the way we expect."

"A different kind of science," I repeat, unsure.

"Neurologists look at structure," she says. "Is there a tumor? A bleed? Damage to the brain tissue? So far, all of your structural tests are coming back clear. That's good news in terms of life-threatening things." She pauses. "But it doesn't mean nothing is happening. It means the problem might be in function. How your brain and nervous system are communicating."

Dad shifts. "So, you're saying his brain is… misfiring?" he asks.

"In a way," she says. "Think about a fire alarm. It's supposed to go off when there's smoke and flames. But sometimes, it goes off when someone burns toast. The alarm is loud. It's annoying. It feels like an emergency, even if the house isn't actually on fire."

I picture the school hallway, the sirens, and the hospital bed.

"Right now," she continues, "we think Rett's nervous system might be acting like an overly sensitive alarm. Something—maybe stress, fear, a past event, or even a pattern his body fell into—might have trained his brain to see danger where there isn't any. And his body responds with very real symptoms: dizziness, fainting, pain."

"So, he's not doing this on purpose," Mom says quietly.

"Absolutely not," Dr. Morales says. "Functional symptoms are not faked. They're not attention, seeking.

They're the nervous system trying, and failing, to protect the person. It's a glitch in how the signals are being sent and interpreted."

The word *glitch* reminds me of what I said to Patch.

I'm a glitch.

Except when she says it, it doesn't sound like an insult. It sounds like… something that can maybe be debugged.

"So, what do we do?" I ask.

"We start by learning," she says. "I'll spend some time talking with you—just us—about what's been happening in your life the last year or two. Not because we're searching for some dramatic cause,' but because sometimes patterns show up when we look at the whole picture."

"So, therapy," I say.

"Therapy," she agrees. "But also, education. We'll talk about Functional Neurological Disorder—FND for short—what it is, how it works, and most importantly, how people get better from it. Because people *do* get better. Not instantly, not magically—but with support, strategies, and time."

The word *better* hooks somewhere behind my ribs.

Dad clears his throat. "Is this… official?" he asks. "A diagnosis?"

"Not yet," Dr. Morales says. "We're still pulling pieces together. However, we are close to deciding that this is the cause. Neurology will rule out a few more things. I'll spend more time with Rett. But FND is very much on the table as an explanation. And if that's what this is, then we have a path forward."

I chew on that.

A path forward.

Not a cure in a pill. Not a surgery that fixes everything in a neat before and after.

But not a void, either.

"Does having this mean I'm… weaker than other people?" I ask, hating how small my voice gets.

She meets my eyes. "It means your brain is sensitive," she says. "And right now, it's been through a lot. Some kids get broken bones. Some get asthma. Some get migraines. Some get nervous systems that decide to freak out in really dramatic ways. None of them are weak. They're just dealing with different battles."

I look at Mom and Dad.

Mom's eyes are wet, but there's something steadier in them now. Dad still looks like he wants to punch a wall, but he's not arguing. He's listening.

"I'm not going to force you to talk about anything you're not ready for today," Dr. Morales says. "We can start small. We can go slow. For now, I mostly wanted you to know: you're not crazy. You're not making this up. And there are a lot of kids like you who've walked through this and come out the other side with their lives back."

I feel something loosen in my chest.

Not all the way. Not even close.

But a little.

"Okay," I say finally. "We can… try it. I guess."

A real, small smile touches her face. "That's all I'm asking for today," she says. "A 'we can try.'"

She stands, smoothing her blazer. "I'll come back this afternoon, if that's alright. Maybe we can talk just the two of us for a bit."

I nod.

"Nice to meet you, Rett," she says, and she actually sounds like she means it.

When she leaves, the room feels weirdly bigger. Like someone opened a window I didn't know was painted shut.

Mom exhales, wiping at her cheeks. "How do you feel about all that?" she asks.

I stare at the monitor, still beeping calmly beside me, as if none of this is a big deal.

"I don't know yet," I say honestly. "I'm glad it's not a tumor. I hate that it might be my own brain doing this. I'm scared they're wrong. I'm scared they're right. And I'm really tired of hospitals."

Dad lets out a breath that's half laugh, half sob. "That sounds about right," he says.

He reaches for my hand, and Mom does too, and suddenly all three of us are tangled together over the blanket, like some weird, lopsided knot.

For a second, I let myself lean into it.

Into them.

Into the possibility that maybe this isn't the beginning of the end.

Maybe it's the beginning of something else.

Not the answer I wanted.

Not the enemy I expected.

But a name for the nothing.

A shape to the fear.

A path, however messy and unfair and exhausting, that doesn't end in sirens.

And this time, it doesn't feel like "for now, that has to be enough."

It feels like the very first step toward whatever comes next.

Chapter 13 – The First Step

Morning filters through the blinds in thin stripes. It isn't bright. It isn't soft. It is just there. A kind of gray light that feels like it belongs in hospital rooms and waiting areas and all the places where time slows down but refuses to stop.

I open my eyes slowly. My head does not throb the way it did last night. It feels more like a bruise. Tender and dull and tired. My body feels heavier than usual. Not the collapsing kind of heavy but the kind that makes you sink deeper into the bed because everything around you is too much.

Mom is curled up in the chair again. Her legs pulled to her chest under a hospital blanket. Her eyes are puffy. Her hair is a mess. She has that look she gets when she has cried more than she would ever admit.

Dad is awake. Sitting by the window with his elbows on his knees. His hands are clasped together and he stares at the floor like it holds every answer he has been begging for. He looks older in this light. More worn down.

I clear my throat. It comes out dry.

Dad looks up instantly. Mom sits forward like someone pressed a button under her.

"Hey" Dad says. He tries to smile but it is tired and stretched thin. "How are you feeling this morning?"

I lie without thinking.

"Okay I guess."

Mom crosses over to me. Her hand goes to my forehead. She checks my temperature even though she knows it isn't that kind of illness. She does it anyway because it is the one thing she can still do.

"You scared us yesterday. The collapse at school, the ambulance, back in the hospital." she whispers.

I look away.

"I scared me too."

Nobody answers that. The room settles back into quiet.

A nurse comes in with vitals. The cuff squeezes my arm and the pulse ox clicks around my finger. She asks how my pain is and I give her a number that sounds brave enough to keep her calm but not so brave she thinks I am fine.

She leaves. The door clicks. Mom exhales.

"What happens now" I ask.

Dad rubs the back of his neck. "The psychologist should be here this morning. And the neurologist is coming by again. They want to see how you are after yesterday."

The word psychologist sits in the air like dust that refuses to fall. None of us move it away.

I pick at the blanket. My fingers tremble. I hate that they tremble.

"Do you think I am crazy" I ask quietly.

Mom's face breaks. Completely. She sits on the edge of the bed and takes my hand in both of hers.

"No. Never. I hate that you even ask that."

Dad shakes his head. "No one thinks that. Not the doctors. Not us. Not anyone. We already told you that. Remember?"

But the truth is heavier than their voices. It settles behind my ribs. The fear sticks anyway.

A soft knock comes from the doorway.

"Morning" Patch says.

My chest loosens at the sight of him without my permission. It just does. He steps inside like he always does. Quiet. Gentle. Present without taking up space.

"You look better sitting up" he says.

"Looks are deceiving" I mutter.

He pulls the same chair he always uses up to the side of the bed. He sits with one ankle resting on his knee. His badge shifts slightly. The name I don't know him by glints in the light.

Patrick Schwartz.

Mom moves aside but she does not leave. Dad stays at the window.

Patch glances between them then back at me.

"You had a hard night" he says.

"Understatement" I reply.

He nods. He never rushes me. He never fills the silence just to fill it. He lets me take the next step on my own.

"I heard what the doctor said yesterday" he says finally. "About the tests. About ruling things out."

I swallow. "About me being the problem."

Patch's eyes soften. "He didn't say that."

"He didn't have to" I whisper.

Patch leans forward slightly but not enough to crowd me.

"Rett. Listen. Your symptoms are real. Your fear is real. Your pain is real. Nothing about what you are going through is pretend. And nothing about it is your fault."

I look down at my hands again. The blanket blurs for a moment. My throat tightens.

"If it is FND" he continues "that does not mean you imagined this. It means your brain and your body got stuck reacting to something that felt dangerous. And now it has trouble shutting off the alarm. But there is a path out of it. It is slow. It is frustrating. It isn't fair. But it is real."

I let the words sit with me. They feel too big. Too heavy. Too hopeful.

Mom wipes her eyes. Dad clears his throat.

Patch gives me a small smile. "You don't have to decide how you feel about it today. You get to take your time."

Before I can answer another knock breaks across the room.

A woman steps inside. Dark hair. Professional clothes. Calm eyes. The same woman from yesterday.

Dr. Morales.

"Good morning, everyone" she says softly. "Rett. Is it alright if I come in"

I nod.

Mom stands. “Do you want us to stay or step out”

My throat clenches. Part of me wants them close. Part of me wants them gone. Part of me does not know what I want.

Dr. Morales saves me from choosing too fast.

“We can start together” she says gently. “And if you want to talk privately at any point you can tell me.”

She pulls the visitor chair closer and sits across from me. Patch stays near the wall. He is here but he gives the moment to her.

“Rett” she says “I want to talk with you about what yesterday meant. Not the collapse. The conversation afterward.”

I nod once. My chest feels tight.

“You heard a lot of information that was overwhelming” she says. “Some of it made sense. Some of it probably made you angry. Some of it probably scared you.”

All of that is true.

I take a breath. “I don’t know what to think.” My voice shakes. “Part of me is relieved it isn’t a tumor. And part of me hates that it might be something wrong with how my brain works. And part of me is scared the doctors are wrong. And part of me is scared they are right."

She nods slowly. "Those are all normal feelings. You don't have to pick one. Your mind is trying to make sense of something that does not feel fair."

A silence follows. Not uncomfortable. Just full.

She leans in slightly.

"Would you be willing to talk with me alone for a few minutes" she asks.

Mom squeezes my shoulder. Dad gives me a small nod.

Patch stays still.

I look at each of them. One by one.

Then I nod.

Mom kisses my forehead and steps out. Dad follows her. They close the door behind them.

Patch stands but he does not leave the room. He stays in the corner and looks at me like he is making sure I can breathe without being watched too closely.

Dr. Morales waits until the door settles before speaking again.

"Rett" she says gently. "Tell me about the last year. Tell me about school. About football. About whatever you lost before the symptoms started."

The words hit somewhere deep.

I blink hard.

"I lost everything" I whisper. "My team. My friends. The version of myself that felt normal. I feel like I am disappearing."

She nods. "That is where we begin."

Something inside me shifts. Something small. Something trembling.

But it is movement.

It is the first step.

When the session ends, I am exhausted. Not physically. Emotionally. Like I emptied something out and left it on the floor between us.

Dad comes back in first. Mom follows.

"How did it go" Mom asks.

I think about the question.

Then I answer honestly.

"I don't understand everything yet. But I think this is the first time I feel like someone knows how to help."

Mom covers her mouth. Dad exhales through his hands.

Steady. Strong.

And somewhere in all the confusion and fear and exhaustion something opens inside me.

It is direction.

A path that is messy and uneven and unfair but still a path.

For the first time in a long time, I am not falling.

I am moving.

And even if not everything makes sense yet, something finally does.

I am not alone.

Chapter 14 – The Girl in the Yellow Cap

I wake up to the sound of my own breathing. Slow. Uneven. Too loud in the quiet hospital room. Mom is curled in the chair beside me with a blanket tucked under her chin. Her phone rests in her hand like she fell asleep scrolling through updates or texting people who want to hear good news that does not exist yet.

My body feels heavy. My head feels foggy. I am tired of staring at ceilings and monitors and the same four walls. Patch has not come by this morning. The nurses floated in earlier to check my vitals and change my IV bag, but even that felt like more of the same. The same routine. The same questions. The same answers that never lead anywhere new.

I need to move or I will lose my mind.

I slide out of bed quietly so I don't wake Mom. The tile is cold under my feet. I steady myself, waiting for the dizziness to pass, then grab the rail along my wall and inch toward the hallway. My body protests, but not enough to stop me. I slip out and take a slow breath. The halls feel wider than they did the day before. Softer. Less like a cage.

Maybe if I walk, I will feel human again.

I don't have a destination at first. I just move. Left at the nurses' station. Right past the mural with painted clouds. Forward until I see the small glass door Patch showed me earlier.

The Commons.

I haven't been here since the day that Patch brought me here. The day that we played Madden and Fortnite.

I push the door open.

Warm air greets me.

Popcorn. I smell popcorn. Real popcorn. It seems impossible, but the scent is unmistakable.

My eyes drift to the couches.

That is when I see her.

A girl sits cross legged on the big couch closest to the television. She has a giant bowl of popcorn in her lap. She is wearing a soft yellow cap that covers her head. It is the kind of yellow that demands attention without yelling. The kind of yellow that looks warm even in winter. Her legs are tucked under her. A blanket covers her lap. Her posture is relaxed. Like she owns the room without trying. Like she knows exactly who she is and does not have time to pretend otherwise.

She is watching the screen with total focus, mouthing the words to herself. I glance at the movie. I recognize it immediately.

Bridge to Terabithia.

I stand there longer than I mean to.

She notices me.

Her head tilts slightly. Her eyes brighten in a way that feels intentional and effortless.

"You want to watch with me?" she asks.

Her voice is soft but confident. She scoots over without waiting for my answer, making room on the couch as if we have known each other longer than the five seconds I have spent staring at her.

I swallow.

"Is it okay?" I ask.

She smiles. It is small. Simple. Honest. The kind of smile that feels real all the way through.

"Of course it is okay. Nobody owns the couch." She pats the cushion beside her. "Except maybe me, but I am generous."

I almost laugh. Not fully. Not out loud. But something in my chest shifts. Something tight loosens just enough for me to breathe differently.

I sit down.

The couch sinks under my weight. She pulls her blanket to the side and offers me the corner seat without a word. I hesitate. I accept and join her on the couch.

The movie continues, but I am more aware of her than the screen.

On the TV, Leslie and Jesse run through the woods toward the rope swing that leads into their secret world. Leslie shouts something just before she swings across the creek.

"Close your eyes but keep your mind wide open."

She mouths the line perfectly, smiling like it is a piece of her.

"That is my favorite part," she whispers.

I glance at her.

"Why?" I ask.

She taps her fingers on her knee as she thinks.

"Because it is true. You don't need everything to be perfect to escape for a little while. You just have to let yourself imagine something better." She shrugs softly. "And sometimes imagining something better is the only way you get through the day."

The answer lands somewhere deep in me.

"Is this your favorite movie?" I ask.

She nods without taking her eyes off the screen.

"It is the best. It makes sad things beautiful." She pauses. "And it makes lonely things feel less lonely." She glances at me briefly. "Leslie is the kind of person I wish I could be. Brave. Bright. Impossible to dim."

There is a pause, "It is harder to be those things when you know time isn't guaranteed." She finishes.

I look at her yellow cap. Her relaxed shoulders. Her expression that holds light even in a building built on fear.

"You kind of remind me of her," I say before I can stop myself.

Her smile widens just slightly. Enough to tell me the comment mattered.

"What is your name?" she asks.

"Rett."

"I am Liz."

The name fits her. Bright. Short. Soft. Strong.

Liz.

She looks back at the screen. I do too. For a few minutes, we sit in comfortable silence. Easy silence. The kind of silence that does not need to be filled.

Leslie builds Terabithia with Jesse, showing him how to turn ordinary branches into kingdoms, creeks into moats, fears into adventures. Liz leans forward slightly during that part. Watching her watch it feels like watching someone remember their own dream.

"That scene always gets me," she whispers. "She is so alive."

I nod.

"Yeah," I say. "She is."

Liz shifts, tucking one leg under her again.

"You come to the Commons much?" she asks.

"Not really."

"You should." She smiles again. "It makes the days feel less like days. More like pieces of something better."

I nod, but I am thinking of something else.

For the first time in months, surrounded by kids who should be sad but are playing games and watching movies and laughing from couches that hide their pain, I don't feel like I am dying.

Blake Collins

I feel like I am here.

And maybe, just maybe, here is enough.

Chapter 15 – What Fear Doesn't Get

Time does not move the same way anymore.

Days blur together until I cannot tell where one ends and the next begins. Weeks pass without clear markers. No weekends. No school bells. Just doctors rotating through my room, whiteboards filling up with names and times, and the slow shift of sunlight across the floor that tells me another day is almost over.

Tests come and go. More scans. More wires. More questions asked gently, then asked again by someone new. Every answer feels incomplete. Every explanation ends with the same words.

We're still trying to understand.

We're trying to help with what's happening in your nervous system.

Therapy becomes part of the routine. Physical therapy in the mornings. Occupational therapy later in the day. And then there is just therapy with Dr. Morales. They guide me through movements that feel foreign, like my body forgot its own instructions. When the symptoms flare, they stop. When they fade, they push a little harder. No one promises anything anymore. They just keep showing up.

I stop counting days.

I start counting visits instead.

The Commons becomes the place I look forward to.

It isn't fancy. Not special, really. But it does not feel like a hospital room either. No beeping machines. No stiff chairs lined against the wall. Just couches pushed together like someone tried to make the space feel intentional, a TV mounted too high, and a microwave that smells permanently like buttered popcorn.

There is always noise in here. Low laughter. The hum of the vending machine. A game console beeping when someone loses. Sometimes a kid cries in the corner. Sometimes someone cheers like they forgot where they are.

I like that.

Liz meets me there most days.

Sometimes it is loud in here. Sometimes it is quiet. But Liz always seems to find me anyway.

Some days we watch movies. Old ones. Sad ones. Ones she already knows by heart and mouths along with like she is afraid they will disappear if she does not. Sometimes she makes me guess the ending just to laugh when I get it wrong.

Sometimes we don't hang at all.

Just sit.

Knees touching.

Our shoulders leaning in without thinking about it.

She steals my popcorn. I pretend to be mad. She never believes me.

Patch will wander through and toss out some joke about us taking over the couch. Liz always rolls her eyes at him like she has known him for years, not weeks. I like that. I like that she belongs here.

There is something about having a place where someone expects you.

Even when nothing else in your life feels certain.

Sometimes she gets there first and claims the good spot on the couch. Sometimes I beat her and stretch out like I won something. We never make a big deal out of it. We just sit down, like this is where we are supposed to be.

The first thing I notice one afternoon isn't her smile.

It is the cap.

It is different than the one she usually wears. Dark blue this time, pulled lower on her forehead, like she is daring anyone to comment on it.

"You switch it up?" I ask, nodding at it as I sit down.

She smirks. "What, you don't like my fashion choices?"

"I didn't say that," I say. "Just… noticing."

She studies me for a second, then shrugs. "Different treatment week."

I don't push. I have learned silence usually works better than questions.

She reaches for the popcorn and shoves it into the microwave. "I have been sick," she says casually, like she is talking about the weather. "It has been a whole thing."

The statement lands heavier than I expect.

"Oh," I say. "I didn't—"

"It is okay," she says quickly. "You are not being weird about it."

The microwave hums, loud in the pause that follows.

"How long?" I ask.

"Long enough that I stopped counting in months," she says. "Surgery once. Radiation after. Now it is more of a… let's see what today feels like situation."

"That sounds exhausting," I say.

She snorts. "That is one word for it."

We carry the popcorn back to the couch and sit down, knees almost touching. She flicks on the TV and scrolls through options like none of it really matters.

"They never like giving straight answers," she adds. "Just percentages. Possibilities. A lot of 'we will monitor it.'"

My ribs ache from familiarity, "Yeah. I know that language."

She glances at me. "They don't know what is wrong with you, do they?"

I shake my head. "They keep finding nothing. Which somehow feels worse. They are pretty sure it is neurological. Something with how my nervous system is reacting."

She nods slowly. "Because an empty scan and blood tests don't explain the pain."

"Exactly."

She leans back into the couch cushions. "Here is the thing nobody tells you," She says. "You can be really sick even when nobody can agree on why. And you don't owe anyone proof that you are hurting."

I stare at the TV, pretending to watch. A laugh track erupts at the wrong moment.

"Does it scare you?" I ask quietly. "Not knowing how it ends?"

She is quiet for a moment.

"Sometimes," she admits. "Mostly it just makes me stubborn."

I glance at her. "Stubborn how?"

"Like… if my body is going to do whatever it wants, I am not going to waste the good days being afraid of the bad ones."

I let that sit for a second. It sounds simple when she says it, but it does not feel simple at all.

"How do you do that?" I ask. "I mean… stay like this. You don't act scared. Or angry. Or tired of everything."

She finally looks at me then. Really looks at me.

"Oh, I am," she says. "All the time."

That surprises me.

"I just figured out that being miserable in advance does not protect you," she continues. "It does not soften the fall. It just steals time you don't get back."

I swallow. "So, you just… decide not to think about it?"

She shakes her head. "No. I think about it. I just don't let it drive."

She pulls her knees up, hugging them loosely.

"There is this lie people tell you," She says quietly. "That if you stay positive, you are strong. And if you are scared, you are failing."

I nod. I have felt that pressure. The constant expectation to be brave. To be grateful. To be okay.

"That isn't how it works," she says. "Some days I am terrified. Some days I am angry. Some days I cannot stand my own body."

Her voice softens.

"But the good days?" she adds. "They are still mine."

I watch her hands twist the edge of the popcorn bag.

"I don't owe my fear the best parts of me," she says. "If my time is going to be limited, then I get to decide what fills it."

The words land heavy and quiet.

"So yeah," she finishes, glancing back at the TV like she didn't just say something huge. "I am not positive. I am intentional."

Something in my chest loosens. Not hope. Not relief.

Permission.

We sit there for a while after that. Not talking. Just existing in the space. The Commons empties out slowly as the afternoon fades. Someone leaves a blanket behind. Someone else forgets their water bottle.

Patch passes by once, pauses in the doorway, then keeps walking.

I don't feel abandoned.

I feel trusted.

I lean back against the couch, letting Liz's words settle into me.

Maybe staying alive isn't about pretending you are okay.

Maybe it is about choosing where you put your attention while you are still here.

And for the first time since I got sick, I realize something quietly important.

Fear does not get to decide everything.

Some parts still belong to me.

Chapter 16 – The Smallest Good Things

The days stop feeling like emergencies.
They still feel serious. They still feel fragile. But the constant edge dulls a little, like my body finally learned how to exhale without waiting for punishment.

I am still in the hospital.

Sometimes I forget that until a nurse comes in to check my blood pressure or the IV pump beeps like it needs attention more than I do. Sometimes I remember it the second I wake up and see the ceiling tiles, the whiteboard with my name written in dry erase marker, the glow of the monitor beside my bed.

But there are stretches now where I don't think about dying.

That feels like progress.

Not the kind you can measure on a chart.

The kind you feel in your bones.

By the second week, Dr. Morales stops saying things like "we are exploring" and "we are learning," and starts saying things like "notice what happens when you don't fight the symptom." She teaches me to name the sensations before I panic.

Lightheaded.

Tight chest.

Buzzing behind my eyes.

A wave.

She teaches me to let it crest and pass instead of gripping the edge of it until it becomes something bigger.

It isn't easy.

Some days it feels like trying to convince a storm not to be a storm.

Other days, it works.

Physical therapy becomes its own kind of humiliation.

They have me stand.

Sit.

Stand again.

Walk five steps.

Stop.

Breathe.

Repeat.

The first time I wobble, my whole-body braces, waiting for the floor to rise up and meet me.

It does not.

My legs shake anyway, angry at the idea of trust.

When I tell the therapist I feel stupid, she does not argue.
She just says, "Your nervous system is relearning. You're not stupid. You're rebuilding."

I hate that word.

Rebuilding.

It sounds like something broken.

But maybe that is the point.

Maybe broken isn't an insult.

Maybe it is just a place you start from.

On the days I can, I go to the Commons.

Patch does not escort me like the first time. He just points with his chin when he sees me in the hallway and says, "You know the way."

The door is always slightly warm when I push it open.

The room smells like popcorn and something sweet, like someone microwaved cookies at some point and the scent never really left. The TV is almost always on, volume low. The couches are worn in the middle, like the room has been carrying people for a long time.

It should make me sad.

But it does not.

It makes me feel less alone.

Liz is there more often than not.

Sometimes she is on the big couch with her legs tucked under her. Sometimes she is in the chair closest to the window, a blanket draped over her lap like a cape. The yellow cap is usually on, soft and bright against the pale hospital colors.

The first time I walk in and see her, she lifts a hand like we are regulars at the same place.

Like we belong here.

"Hey," she says.

"Hey," I say back.

That is all it takes to make my chest loosen.

We don't start with deep conversations.

We start with dumb ones.

She asks me what my worst class is, and I say English just to get a reaction. She gasps like I slapped her.

"Liar," she says. "You look like the type who gets As in English and hates it."

"I do hate it," I admit.

She smiles like she won.

We argue about movies.

Not important arguments.

The kind you can win and lose without bleeding.

She says Bridge to Terabithia is the saddest movie ever made. I say she is being dramatic. She tells me I am emotionally repressed.

"You don't even know me," I say.

"I know enough," she replies, and tosses popcorn at my chest.

It hits the front of my hoodie and drops into my lap.

I stare at it.

"You littered on me," I say.

"It's biodegradable," she says, like that solves everything.

I laugh.

It surprises me how easy it comes out, how it does not hurt my head, how it does not make me dizzy, how my body does not punish me for it.

Liz notices.

She tilts her head slightly, studying me like she is reading something written between my ribs.

"What?" I ask, defensive.

"Nothing," she says. Then, quieter, "You look like you forgot you could do that."

"Do what?"

She shrugs, but her eyes stay on mine.

"Be a kid."

The words land hard.

Not because they are dramatic.

Because they are true.

I look away, suddenly interested in the TV.

The screen shows a cartoon character falling down in an over exaggerated way. A laugh track erupts. The room stays warm. Someone across the Commons groans when they lose a game.

Normal sounds.

Normal things.

The smallest good things.

I don't realize my leg is bouncing until Liz reaches out and presses her hand lightly against my knee.

Not to stop it.

Just to let me know she noticed.

"Hey," she says again, softer this time.

I look at her.

"Your body's doing that thing," she says. "The runaway thought thing."

I swallow.

"What if I pass out?" I ask quietly.

Liz's expression does not change.

No pity.

No panic.

Just her.

"Then you pass out," she says. "And someone helps you. And you wake up. And you get mad. And you keep living."

My throat tightens.

Because she says it like it is the simplest math in the world.

"That's easy for you to say," I mutter.

She snorts. "No, it's not."

And then she looks at me, really looks at me, and her voice shifts into something more honest.

"My body tries to kill my hair," she says. "Your body tries to take you out like an iPhone at one percent."

I blink.

She smiles, faint but real. "Bodies are rude."

I laugh again.

Bigger this time.

Liz watches me like she is saving the sound for later.

When the laugh fades, something quieter sits in its place.

Relief.

Not because I am fixed.

Not because anything is solved.

Because for the first time in months, my life isn't just symptoms and fear and waiting rooms.

For the first time in months, there is a couch.

A movie.

A bowl of popcorn.

A girl in a yellow cap making jokes like the world is still worth teasing.

And somehow, in the middle of all that noise and plastic smell and fluorescent light, my body does something it has not done in a long time.

It rests.

Not fully.

Not perfectly.

But enough.

Enough to make me think maybe this is how you come back.

Not with miracles.

Not with a switch flipping.

With the smallest good things, stacked on top of each other, until they start to feel like a life again.

Chapter 17 – The Days That Stayed

The days after that begin to stack quietly.

Not in a way that feels important at first. There are no milestones. No announcements. Just small, ordinary hours piling up on each other until they start to feel like something solid.

I am still inpatient.

Liz is still coming to the Commons.

Patch still pretends he does not know all of our routines.

And for the first time in weeks, nothing is falling apart.

Most mornings I wake to the same ceiling and the same soft knock on the door. Nurses come and go. Vitals. Clipboards. Gentle voices asking how I slept. I answer. They write things down. Life continues.

By late morning, I go to the Commons.

Liz is usually already there.

Sometimes she is curled into her chair with her knees tucked beneath her, a book resting half-open in her lap. Other times she is watching something ridiculous on the TV, laughing at jokes that are not even funny. Occasionally she is asleep when I arrive, her head tipped to one side, the brim of her knit cap shadowing her eyes.

I never wake her.

I sit instead.

That becomes our thing.

Not talking right away. Not needing to fill the space. Just being in the same room, breathing the same air.

When she wakes, she always looks a little startled to see me, like she forgot she invited me into her day. And then she smiles, soft and slow, and it feels like I have arrived somewhere important.

"You're early," she says once.

"Or you're late," I reply.

She laughs. That sound still catches me off guard. It is lighter than everything else in this building.

Some days we play games. Card games. Old video games. Uno until she beats me so badly I accuse her of cheating.

Some days we don't hang at all.

We sit with a movie on. We half-watch it. We talk about scenes like they matter more than they do. We make fun of bad acting. We root for characters we know are going to lose.

Sometimes she tells me about home.

About her dog who still sleeps in her room even though she isn't there. About a swing set in her backyard that squeaks in the wind. About her grandma's sewing room, full of fabric and thread and little glass jars of buttons that don't match.

I tell her about football.

About the field at sunset. The way the grass smells right before a game. About how loud everything gets when you are in the middle of a play and how quiet it feels right after.

"You miss it," she says once.

"Yeah," I admit. "But I don't feel broken about it anymore."

She looks at me like she is proud of that.

She shifts on the couch, tugging her blanket higher around her shoulders.

"Did you have a spring formal or something this year?" she asks suddenly.

"Yeah," I say. "Prom is in a few weeks."

She makes a small sound in her throat, halfway between a laugh and a shrug.

"Figures," she says. "I was supposed to go this year."

"Were you?" I ask.

"Mm-hmm." She watches the screen, not really watching it. "I even had a dress picked out. Yellow, actually. My mom still has it hanging in my closet like it's waiting for me to come home."

There's a quiet stretch after that.

"I told her not to keep it," she adds softly. "It feels silly now. Like pretending things didn't change."

I don't know what to say, so I don't say anything.

Liz tilts her head toward me.

"Hey," she says lightly, like she's fixing it before it can break. "It's fine. I just thought it was funny."

But the way she looks back at the screen tells me it isn't.

By the end of the week, something has changed.

Not in my body.

In my chest.

I stop waiting for something bad to happen every second we are together. I stop scanning her face for signs that she is fading. I stop measuring every moment like it might be the last.

I start letting them just be moments.

One afternoon, she looks especially tired. Her shoulders droop. Her smile comes slower.

"Want to go back to your room?" I ask.

She shakes her head. "I like it here."

"Even when you feel bad?"

"Especially then."

So we stay.

She falls asleep halfway through a movie. This time her head tips toward me.

It is small. Light. Careful.

I don't move.

For the first time since I got sick, I am not afraid of stillness.

Patch passes by and pretends not to notice.

Her hand shifts in her sleep, brushing against mine. I feel it like a pulse.

When she wakes, she does not pull away.

"Did I drool on you?" she asks.

"Tragically," I say.

She grins.

Later, when a nurse calls her name, she squeezes my fingers before standing.

"I'll be back," she says.

"I know," I tell her.

And I do.

She always comes back.

Until one day, she does not.

I tell myself it's nothing.

Kids miss days. Treatments run long. People get tired.

Still, when I wake the next morning, something in my chest already feels off.

The ceiling looks the same. The soft knock still comes. Nurses still ask their questions. Life keeps moving like it always does.

But when I think about the Commons, I don't picture her smile.

I picture the space beside me.

I picture her chair.

Empty.

I shake it off.

It has only been one morning.

She will be there by lunch.

She always is.

Blake Collins

Chapter 18 – The Shape of Missing

The days slow down after that.

Not in a dramatic way. Not in a way anyone warns you about. They just stretch. Thin. Uneventful. Long enough that I stop counting them and start measuring time by meals and vitals and whether the sun is coming through the window or not.

I'm still inpatient.

They say it's for safety. Because my symptoms are unpredictable. Because I passed out at school. Because they want to make sure, I can manage things before they send me home again.

I don't argue. I'm too tired to.

In the mornings, nurses come in with clipboards and quiet voices. They ask the same questions in slightly different orders.

How's your pain today?
Any dizziness when you stand?
Any nausea?
Any anxiety?
Do you feel safe?

I answer because that's what you do when people ask you things with concern in their eyes. I rate my pain on a scale that never quite fits. I nod when they explain things

I've already heard. I watch them write things down and leave.

By late morning, there is nothing to do but wait.

Patch visits. He suggests the Commons.

It feels like the only place in the hospital that doesn't expect anything from me.

So, I go.

The room looks the same as it always does. The couches are pushed together near the TV. The game console hums softly. A puzzle sits half-finished on the table like someone stopped mid thought. The popcorn smell lingers, faint but familiar.

Her chair is empty.

I stop just inside the doorway without realizing it.

It's stupid. I know that. People aren't assigned seats here. Kids come and go. Schedules change. Treatments change. People disappear and reappear all the time.

Still, I notice.

I take the controller and sit on the couch instead. I turn on a game I have played a hundred times. I pick a team without really thinking about it. My fingers move automatically, muscle memory doing most of the work.

Five minutes in, I realize I have no idea what the score is.

I quit and put on a movie instead. Something loud and fast that is supposed to distract me. The kind of thing Patch would usually make fun of while pretending not to care.

The screen flashes. People talk. Something explodes.

I watch all of it and none of it.

Every few minutes, my eyes drift back to the doorway.

She doesn't come.

I stay longer than I mean to. Long enough that the room empties out. Long enough that the noise fades and I am left with the hum of the TV and the quiet reminder that I am still here.

Back in my room, the afternoon crawls.

A doctor stops by. Another set of questions. Another careful explanation about plans and next steps. Neurology is still reviewing. Dr. Morales will be involved. We are looking at the whole picture.

I stare at the wall and nod.

Later, someone comes in with a worksheet. Breathing exercises. Grounding techniques. Ways to notice your body without panicking.

I try because they ask me to.

It feels like being told to calm down while you are drowning.

That night, I dream about the Commons.

Not anything specific. Just the room. The sound of laughter. A voice I can't quite place. When I wake up, my chest feels tight in a way that has nothing to do with my head.

The next day is more of the same.

Vitals. Questions. Waiting.

I go back to the Commons after lunch.

Her chair is still empty.

I don't sit this time. I just stand there for a second, longer than I should, like I'm expecting the room to explain itself.

No one does.

Patch shows up later and asks if I want to play something. I tell him maybe later. He nods like he understands and doesn't push.

That is one of his skills.

By the third day, the absence feels heavier.

I catch myself listening for her laugh before I even enter the room. Catch myself scanning faces that aren't hers. Catch myself thinking about something dumb I could say if she were there.

It's strange how quickly quiet becomes noticeable when it wasn't before.

The doctors keep coming. The questions keep looping. I start answering before they finish asking. I start shortening my responses. My head hurts. A little. Not too bad. I am dizzy sometimes. I am tired all the time.

Yes. No. Maybe. I don't know.

At night, I think about Liz.

I wonder if she got discharged. If she is home. If she is better. If she just got bored of the Commons and found somewhere else to sit.

I tell myself it doesn't matter.

But it does.

On the fourth day, I go to the Commons again without really deciding to. It feels like habit now. Like gravity.

The room is busier than it has been all week. A couple kids are arguing over a controller. Someone is laughing too loud at something on the TV. Patch is leaning against the wall, talking to a nurse.

Aliza.

His wife.

And just like that.

She's back.

Same chair. Same spot. Like nothing had changed at all.

She looks up when she hears the door.

For half a second, our eyes meet, and something in my chest loosens before I can stop it.

But then I take another step into the room.

And I notice the difference.

It's not anything obvious. Not at first. She's still wearing the same kind of hoodie she always does. Still sitting with one knee pulled up, hands tucked into the sleeves like she's trying to stay warm. Still with a head wrap tied in a knot, excess cascading down her shoulders.

But her skin looks paler than I remember.

Like the color drained a little while she was gone and hasn't quite found its way back yet.

Her eyes are the same. Bright. Curious. Hazel. But there's a tiredness underneath them I don't remember seeing before. The kind that doesn't go away with sleep.

She lifts a hand in a small wave when she sees me, and I realize her movements are slower. Careful. Like she's measuring how much energy she has before her tank is depleted.

I hesitate. She looks like she's here. But not all the way.

Chapter 19 – The Art of Not Disappearing

For a second, I just stare at her.

Not because she is here.

Because she is different.

The Commons is loud around us. The TV is playing in the corner. Someone laughs too hard at something that isn't that funny. A controller clicks. A nurse calls a name near the doorway.

None of it feels real.

All I can see is Liz, sitting in her chair with that familiar, easy smile, like the last few days never happened.

I sit across from her and try to act normal. Try to match her energy. Try to pretend I didn't notice how empty the room felt while she was gone.

The worry stays hooked in my chest.

It isn't loud.

It isn't panic.

It is the kind of worry that settles in and refuses to leave.

“You look like you have something to say,” she says.

Her voice is soft. Matter of fact. Like she isn’t inviting drama, just honesty.

“I don’t,” I lie. Acting offended.

She raises her eyebrows, clearly not convinced, but she does not call me out. She just waits.

It is frustrating how good she is at that.

“Where were you?” I ask, trying to make it sound casual. Like a joke. Like I have not been counting days.

She looks down at her hands. Her sleeves are pulled over her knuckles. She rubs her thumb along the edge of the fabric, slow and absentminded.

“Not here,” she says.

“Yeah,” I say. “I figured that part out.”

The corner of her mouth lifts, but the smile does not last. She leans her head back against the chair and stares at the ceiling, like she is deciding how much truth to give me.

“I disappear sometimes,” she says. “When it gets bad.”

My stomach tightens.

"Bad how?"

She turns her head toward me. Her eyes are bright and hazel and steady. Even tired, they are steady.

"Chemo," she says.

The word lands between us and does not move.

I blink. "Chemo?" Asking, like I don't understand the meaning of that word.

She nods once, like she is confirming the weather.

"Leukemia," she adds. "I hate that word," she mutters. "It sounds like a sneeze."

Then she looks at me. "I am way cooler than my disease."

I don't react the way I think I am supposed to. I don't gasp. I don't say I am sorry. I don't say that it is terrible.

I just stare at her.

Because she is sitting here like a normal person.

Because she is smiling like she is fine.

Because she isn't.

She glances toward the TV. A kid yells at the screen. Patch laughs at something a nurse says. The noise gives her cover.

"I used to be normal," she says. "Like actually normal. Annoying normal."

I don't know if I should laugh, but she lets out a short breath that sounds like one.

"I was always outside," she continues. "Always doing something. Climbing. Jumping off stuff I probably should not have been jumping off. I had bruises all the time. My mom used to tell me I was going to break a bone one day and she wouldn't be surprised."

Her voice warms as she talks, like she can almost touch that version of herself again.

Then she looks down at her arm.

"There was this one bruise," she says. "Right here. On my forearm. It was nothing. I didn't even remember how I got it. But it wouldn't go away."

I watch her mouth tighten slightly.

"At first I thought it was funny," she says. "Like I finally did something that left a mark."

She pauses.

"Then there were more," she adds. "And they didn't fade. And I started getting tired. Not normal tired. The kind where you can sleep for ten hours and still feel wrecked."

I am lost in her story. Waiting for what comes next. She pauses, "And you told your parents?" I ask.

"Eventually," she says. "I didn't want to. I hate being the reason people worry."

That hits something in me harder than I expect.

She continues on with her story.

There is a pause, a moment of reflection between us.

"It was a nice day," she says. "Spring or summer. Warm. My parents took me to the park because they thought I needed fresh air. Like sunlight was going to refill my energy."

That makes her smile, a real one, and it makes my chest ache.

"I was playing," she says. "Running around like I always do. Trying to prove I was fine."

She looks at me, and I know she realizes that sentence belongs to both of us.

"I got out of breath," she says. "Out of nowhere. Like I couldn't pull enough air in. I bent over with my hands on my knees. My dad told me to slow down. My mom asked if I wanted water."

She swallows.

"Then my nose started bleeding."

I flinch.

"A lot," she adds. "Not a drip. It wouldn't stop. My mom kept handing me tissues and saying it was fine. That it happens. That maybe the air was dry."

Her eyes go distant, like she is back there.

"But it didn't stop," she says quietly. "We tried everything. Pinching it. Ice. Waiting. My dad kept checking his watch like that would help. And then my mom looked at him, and I saw it in her face."

Her voice stays calm, but something tightens beneath it.

"She was scared," she says. "Not worried. Scared."

My fingers curl into the couch cushion.

"And then?" I ask.

"And then we went in," she says. "Urgent care first. They sent us to the ER. They did blood work. Asked a lot of questions. Then they came back with faces that were trying too hard to look normal."

She exhales slowly.

"You ever notice how adults get quiet when they are trying not to panic?" she asks.

I nod.

"I heard my mom crying in the hallway," she says. "I didn't even know why yet. I just heard her. And I knew it was bad."

She pulls her sleeves farther over her hands.

"It is blood cancer," she says. "That is how the doctor said it first. Like maybe saying it that way would soften the blow. Leukemia. I didn't even know how to spell it."

She looks at me again.

"I know you are supposed to say you are sorry," she says. "You don't have to. I am not telling you for that."

"I was going to," I admit. My voice is rough.

"I know," she says. "I just don't want it. I get enough of it."

I nod. I understand that too well.

"Chemo started fast," she says. "There was not much time to think. Just appointments and information and people throwing words around like treatment plan and remission like they were ordering food."

My stomach turns.

"What does it feel like?" I ask. "Chemo."

She does not hesitate.

"Like fire," she says. "I can feel it traveling through my veins. It burns."

The words are simple. Flat. Honest.

"Like something burning and moving through my entire body." She speaks. "Sometimes it is slow and just sits there. Other times it hits all at once and it feels like my whole body is screaming. And after that, I am empty. Like my bones are hollow."

She pauses, her eyes unfocused, voice quieter now. "There are moments when I think death would be kinder than this. When the pain feels endless, and I wonder if letting go would be easier. If I was not so afraid of what comes after, I might even welcome it. Because at least then, it would stop." Her eyes well up with tears.

I look away, knowing that I may begin crying too.

"That is why you were gone," I say.

She nods.

"When it gets bad, I don't come here," she says. "I cannot. I don't want people seeing me like that. And I don't have the energy to pretend."

I look at her again. The paleness. The tiredness. The way her smile does not fully settle.

"You don't have to pretend with me," I say before I can stop myself.

She looks surprised. Then relieved.

"Good," she says. "Because I am really bad at pretending."

We sit there while the room keeps moving around us. It is strange how the world stays loud even after someone says something that should stop time.

She reaches up and touches the edge of her cap. It is soft and knitted, a deep blue that makes her eyes look brighter.

"My grandma makes them," she says. "The hats I mean."

I begin looking at the seam work, the patterns, the simplicity, and the beauty of the one she is wearing.

She continues, "She is a seamstress. She used to make me dresses when I was little. She still calls me her little model."

That makes her smile again, and it lasts longer.

"She said if my hair was going to leave, then I deserved something better than hospital caps," she says. "So, she makes these. In my favorite colors."

"It's nice," I say.

"It is her way of fixing what she cannot fix," she says.

The words settle quietly in my chest.

Liz leans back and studies me.

"Your turn," she says.

"My turn?" I reply.

She shrugs. Matter of fact again.

"What is wrong with you?" she asks. "Not the doctor version. Your version."

My voice catches.

I could lie. I could joke. I could shrug it off.

But she just told me she lives with fire in her veins and still shows up here.

So, I tell the truth.

"It started at football practice," I say.

She listens closely.

"Going into sophomore year," I continue. "One of those days where the air feels thick. Hot. Humid. Like breathing through something wet."

I can smell it again. Sweat. Grass. Sunscreen baking into skin.

"We were running drills," I say. "Sprints. Cuts. Coach yelling like always. Everyone trying to prove something."

My hands are sweating now.

"I was doing good," I admit. "Really good. Fast. Locked in. It felt like everything was finally clicking. Like I could be someone."

She does not interrupt.

"Then I got dizzy," I say. "Just for a second. Like the field shifted. I tried to shake it off."

I swallow.

"My vision blurred," I say. "The sky got too bright. I thought it was heat. I thought it was a lack of water."

I laugh once, but it isn't funny.

"I pushed through," I say. "Because you don't stop. You don't quit. You don't admit something feels wrong."

My voice drops.

"I took one more step," I say. "And then I woke up on the ground."

She nods. No shock. Just understanding.

"They said heat exhaustion," I say. "Everyone acted like it was solved. Coach told me to hydrate. My parents hovered for a while. And then I was fine."

I pause.

"Not fine," I correct. "Just normal enough that people stopped worrying. The symptoms stayed. Headaches. Dizziness. That tilting feeling. And then it happened again."

I look at her.

"After it happens once," I say, "you start living like it will happen again."

Her mouth tightens.

"Even on good days," I continue. "Even when nothing is wrong. You wait for it. And when things started going really well for me, which is when it got worse."

"Why?" she asks.

"Because I was scared of losing it," I say. "Scared of success. Scared of expectations. Scared of passing out again and ruining everything."

The honesty burns.

"I quit," I say. "Because I couldn't handle waiting for it to happen. I couldn't trust my body anymore."

My chest grows heavy.

"I thought quitting would make the fear go away," I say. "It didn't. It got louder. Football was the thing I loved. The thing that drowned it out. When it was gone, all I had left was watching my friends keep playing without me."

Liz looks down at her hands.

"Yeah," she says.

That one word understands more than any doctor ever has.

We sit there in the noise and the quiet at the same time.

Two people on a couch.

Two bodies that stopped being trustworthy.

Two lives divided by a single normal day.

"I disappear when it gets bad," she says again. "Not because I don't want to be here. Just because I cannot."

"I get that," I say.

She studies me for a moment.

"Then maybe," she says, "we just tell each other when we are disappearing."

It isn't a promise.

It isn't hope.

It is something smaller.

Something real.

"Deal," I say.

Nothing gets lighter. We just stop pretending we are carrying it by ourselves.

Chapter 20 – What Care Looks Like

Some days feel heavier than others.

Not because anything bad happens. Not because someone brings new information or bad news. Just because my body wakes up already tired, like it spent the night holding itself together instead of resting.

On most days, I go to the Commons.

It has become routine without me deciding it should be. Like my feet know where to take me before my brain does.

Liz is there when I walk in.

She is curled into her chair with a blanket pulled over her legs, hoodie sleeves covering her hands. A movie plays on the TV, something animated and loud enough to feel cheerful without asking much in return.

She looks up when she sees me.

"Hey," she says.

"Hey."

That is all. It feels like enough.

I sit on the couch across from her and stretch my legs out. We watch the screen for a while without talking. A character says something ridiculous. Liz lets out a quiet laugh, surprised by it, like she didn't expect herself to react at all.

I notice things I didn't used to.

How she adjusts the blanket more than once. How she shifts positions like she is searching for a version of comfortable that keeps slipping away. How she keeps her shoulders slightly rounded, conserving energy without drawing attention to it.

Halfway through the movie, her head tilts.

At first, I think she is just listening.

Then her eyes close.

She does not lean toward me. She does not slump. She simply drifts, slow and unannounced, like someone dimming a light one notch at a time.

Her breathing evens out.

I stay where I am.

I don't pause the movie. I don't move. I let the moment exist exactly as it is. Unsure of how much time has passed.

When she wakes up, she blinks like she forgot where she was.

"Sorry," she says right away.

"For what?" I ask.

She gestures vaguely. "That."

"You fell asleep," I say.

"So rude of me," she says, completely serious.

I almost smile.

"You were tired," I say.

She shrugs. "I am always tired...especially after treatments."

The way she says it sticks with me. Not alarming. Just honest.

We finish the movie. She stays awake this time, though I can tell it costs her something. When it ends, she stretches and winces before she can stop herself.

"You okay?" I ask.

"Yeah," she says, exhaustion in her voice.

The word settles between us, heavier than it sounds.

Patch wanders over a little later and asks if we want to play something. Liz shakes her head.

"I think I am done for today," she says.

That used to mean disappearing. Back to her room. Back to a place I didn't see.

Today, she stays where she is.

"I can hang out a bit longer," she adds. "Just sitting. No games, we can leave a movie on if we want, but I just want to rest."

"Are you sure?" I ask. "I think you should rest."

I expect her to brush it off. Make a joke. Tell me she is fine.

Instead, she smiles. Not big. Not forced. Just honest.

"I am resting," she says. "I just want to be with you. Here." She nods toward the room. "I hate that room."

I understand immediately.

The quiet. The beeping. The way the walls feel like they are listening. The way time stretches and folds in on itself until you forget what day it is.

"I do too," I say.

She looks at me for a second like she knows I am not just talking about her room.

I think about my own bed. My own ceiling. The way morning light used to hit the floor of my bedroom. I think about waking up without someone checking my vitals. About grabbing a bowl of cereal without asking permission. About being part of a world that does not smell like antiseptic and loss.

Normal feels far away. Like something that belongs to someone else.

We sit quietly after that.

Not awkward. Not heavy. Just still.

People come and go around us. A nurse laughs at something Patch says. A kid runs past chasing another one. The TV plays in the background, forgotten but comforting, like noise from another life.

Liz shifts slightly, settling deeper into the chair. Her eyes close for a second, then open again. She exhales, slow and deliberate.

I notice how careful she is with her energy. How she chooses where to spend it. How being here costs her something and how she decides it is worth it anyway.

I don't tell her she should go lie down. I don't tell her to save her strength.

I let her choose.

And something about that feels important.

We are not talking. We are not fixing anything.

We are just sitting in the same space, refusing to be alone in it.

I realize then that caring does not always look like doing something.

Sometimes it looks like staying quiet.

Sometimes it looks like letting someone stay.

Sometimes it looks like sharing a room and letting it be enough.

For once, my thoughts don't race ahead of the moment. I notice that and let it be.

Later that afternoon, I meet with the psychologist.

She asks how I am doing, which I am starting to understand isn't the same as asking how I feel.

"I think I am okay," I say after a moment. "Not great. But okay."

She nods. "What does okay look like right now?"

I think about Liz falling asleep during the movie. About staying still instead of spiraling. About letting quiet be enough.

"It looks like staying," I say. "Not trying to outrun my body. Not assuming something bad is about to happen just because things feel calm."

She writes something down.

"And how does that feel?" she asks.

I consider it.

"Different," I say. "Lighter, I think."

That answer surprises me.

Before she leaves, she asks, "What has helped?"

I picture Liz again. The way she shows up even when she is exhausted. The way she does not deny what is happening to her body, but does not let it take everything either.

"Someone who understands what it feels like when your body stops cooperating," I say.

She nods. "Connections matters."

When I go back to the Commons that evening, Liz is gone.

I notice the empty chair.

I don't try to explain it away.

The room keeps moving around me. People come and go. The TV shifts to something else. Someone laughs somewhere behind me.

I sit down anyway.

The absence stays.

So, do I.

Chapter 21 – Tethered

The appointment feels different before it even starts.

I notice it while I am sitting in the chair across from her desk, feet flat on the floor, hands resting on my knees. My body is still. Not tense. No pain. No shaking or uneasiness. I'm not waiting for something to go wrong.

Just here.

The psychologist looks at me for a moment before she speaks, like she is taking inventory.

"You look steadier," she says.

"I feel steadier," I tell her.

That feels important.

She nods. "Tell me when you first noticed the change."

I think about it.

Not one moment. Not a switch flipping. Just a slow easing.

"I think it started with Liz," I say. "Being around her."

She waits; lets the silence do its work.

"She has so little time," I continue. "And somehow, she still loves life. Not in a big inspirational way. Just in small things. Bad movies. Popcorn. Sitting in a room with people instead of being alone."

I pause.

"She taught me how to live," I say. "How to enjoy what is right in front of me instead of worrying about what might be taken away."

The psychologist nods again. Not surprised.

"And what were you most afraid of before?" she asks.

"Losing control," I say. "Of my body. Of my life. I wanted to be a kid. To play football. To run around without worrying that I would just drop."

I take a breath.

"But the fear was bigger than football," I add. "It was the fear of not being able to enjoy anything. Of always waiting for my body to ruin it."

"And now?" she asks.

I think about Liz laughing at dumb jokes. About falling asleep in the Commons. About how calm my head feels lately.

"My fear of life disappeared," I say. "The expectations vanished. I stopped trying to be perfect. Liz showed me how to just take life as it comes."

She leans back slightly. Smiling.

"Your symptoms make sense," she says. "Your nervous system learned to stay on high alert after the collapse at practice. Every success became another thing you could lose. Your body tried to protect you by taking control away before something worse could happen."

I listen. Really listen.

"This does not mean you imagined your symptoms," she continues. "They were real. Your body was responding to fear, pressure, and loss of control. What has changed isn't your body. It is your relationship with it."

She pauses, then adds, "Have you ever heard of fainting goats?"

I blink. "No."

"They're goats with a nervous system that reacts too strongly to surprise," she says. "When they get startled, their muscles lock up. They fall over. Not because they're weak. Because their bodies are trying to protect them."

I picture it before I can stop myself. A body choosing stillness over danger.

"They're not broken," she continues. "They don't need to be fixed. They just need safety. Consistency. Time. When they stop expecting danger, their bodies stop reacting so dramatically."

Something settles in my chest.

"Your body did the same thing," she says. "It learned that success, pressure, and unpredictability felt like threats. So, it shut things down to keep you safe."

I nod slowly.

"You stopped running," she says. "You found connection. Purpose. Your nervous system learned it was safe again."

That lands quietly.

"And that is why you are ready to go home," she says.

The words land slowly.

Home.

My room. My bed. My ceiling. Morning light instead of fluorescent bulbs. Waking up without someone checking my vitals before I am fully awake.

The idea fills me with excitement. Real excitement. The kind I have not trusted myself with in a long time.

"I am ready," I say.

"And how does leaving feel?" she asks.

The question catches me off guard.

I open my mouth, prepared with one answer, but then I close it again.

"I am excited," I say. "I really am."

"But…" She says. She could tell there was one coming.

"But I am scared too," I add quietly.

"Of what?" she asks.

I swallow.

"Of leaving her here," I say.

The words feel heavier once they are out.

"She is used to hospitals," I continue. "She knows how this works. She acts like it does not bother her. But when I think about her waking up here and me not being down the hall anymore, it feels wrong. These last few weeks were beneficial, not just to me. It made a difference in her too. I know it did."

I stop for a second. My hands are clenched in my lap. I didn't notice until now.

"It does not make me panic," I say. "It just… hurts. The thought of her being alone in that room when she already spends so much time there. So much time in here."

"That makes sense," she says gently.

"I am not leaving her," I say quickly. "I will come back every day. After school. On weekends. I will bike the two miles if I have to. I just need her to know that I am still here."

She studies me, careful.

"And why is that important to you?" she asks. "Not obligation. Not guilt."

I think about Liz in the Commons. Falling asleep mid movie. Laughing at bad jokes. Choosing to sit in a room full of noise instead of lying alone in bed.

"She is my best friend," I say.

The words come out simple. Obvious. Like they have been waiting for me to finally say them.

"She is the first person in weeks who really saw me," I continue. "Not my symptoms. Not my chart. Just me. And I think I might be the first person who treated her like a kid."

I pause.

"Not a disease," I add quietly. "Not a diagnosis. Just someone who likes bad movies and popcorn and sitting in a loud room because it feels more like life."

I swallow.

"I hate that word," I say. "Cancer. But it is true. And I don't want that to be the only thing people see when they look at her."

I take a breath.

"I can run. I can jump. I can go home. She lost those things. The least I can do is stay present with her while I have them."

The psychologist nods.

"That sounds like care," she says. "Not fear."

When I leave the appointment, the hallway feels different. Not lighter. Just clearer.

I am going home.

And I am leaving someone behind.

Both things are true.

I should go back to my room.
I should pack.
I should do something that looks like preparing.

Instead, my feet carry me toward the Commons.

The Commons smells like popcorn again.

It's faint, like someone made a bag hours ago and the warmth never fully left the room. The lights are softer in here than the rest of the hospital. Not dim, exactly. Just less sharp. Less like they're trying to catch you doing something wrong.

A couple kids are gathered around the TV, laughing at something I can't hear. Someone is coloring at the round table near the window, their head bent low like the world has narrowed down to a handful of markers and a blank page.

Patch spots me the second I walk in.

"Well, well," he says, like I'm late to an appointment. "Look who decided to join society."

"I was busy," I mutter.

"Busy doing what?" he asks, eyebrows lifting. "Staring at the ceiling? Counting the tiles?"

I don't answer, which is answer enough.

Patch grins anyway and goes back to stacking board games on the cart like he's building a wall between me and whatever I'm trying not to feel.

I drift toward the couch, mostly because it's familiar now. The cushions sag in the same places. The fabric is worn down where too many kids have sat in the same spot, needing somewhere soft to land.

That's when I notice him.

He's sitting at the far end of the room near the puzzle table; legs folded beneath him like he's trying to take up as little space as possible. He looks younger than me. Twelve maybe. Thirteen at most. His head is bald, but not in the way Patch's jokes make it seem normal. In the way that makes the truth obvious.

There's an IV pole beside him with a bag hanging from it, and the tubing disappears beneath the sleeve of his hoodie. He doesn't look scared of it. He looks like it's just… part of him. Like an extra limb.

He catches me staring.

Instead of looking away, he lifts his chin slightly and says, "What?"

The word isn't rude. Not really.

It's more like he's tired of being looked at like a question mark.

"Nothing," I say quickly. "Sorry."

He studies me for a second longer than he needs to, then nods toward the table.

"You play anything?" he asks.

I glance down at the board games scattered across the cart. "Depends."

"Uno?" he says.

"Yeah," I answer. "I can do Uno."

He gestures toward the chair across from him like it's obvious I should sit there.

So, I do.

The cards are already out, half shuffled. He deals like he's done it a hundred times in this room, like this is his table and the rest of the hospital just borrowed it.

"What's your name?" he asks, flipping a card into the middle.

"Rett," I say.

"Rett," he repeats, like he's testing it. "That's a football name."

I almost laugh. It's not funny. It's just… accurate.

"Used to be," I say.

He doesn't ask what I mean by that. He just tosses down a yellow six.

"I'm Carter," he says.

"Carter," I repeat.

He nods once, satisfied, and keeps playing.

For a few minutes, the game is just the game. Cards slapping the table. The occasional "skip" and "draw two" that makes him groan like he's personally offended by my existence.

"You're annoying," he says when I hit him with another draw two.

"You started it," I tell him.

He smirks. "I guess."

The atmosphere feels lighter. Just a little.

Then he plays a wild card and changes the color to blue.

"Cheater," I say.

"That's not cheating," he says. "That's strategy."

"You're eleven," I remind him.

"Twelve," he corrects immediately. "And I'm basically a genius."

I shake my head, but I can't stop the small smile that slips out.

Carter sees it and looks pleased with himself, like that was the whole goal.

We keep playing. And somewhere between my third win and his second comeback, the conversation shifts without either of us pushing it.

He glances at the IV pole like it's an afterthought and says, "You live here too?"

I swallow. "Kind of."

"Same," he says easily. "I've been here for a while."

I don't ask how long. I don't want the number.

Instead, I ask the question that feels safer.

"What do you have?" I say quietly.

Carter shrugs like I asked what his favorite color is.

"Leukemia," he answers.

The word lands on the table between us, heavier than the cards.

I stare at him. "Oh."

He tilts his head. "What? You thought I shaved my head for fun?"

"Sorry," I mutter again.

Carter waves a hand like he's brushing it off. "It's fine. People get weird about it."

"Do you… feel okay?" I ask. It's a stupid question. It's the only one I have.

Carter thinks for a second. "Sometimes," he says. "Sometimes I feel like trash. Sometimes I feel normal. Sometimes I feel like both in the same hour."

I nod because I understand that part more than I want to.

"Why are you here?" he asks, eyes narrowing slightly. Not suspicious. Curious.

"I don't know," I admit.

Carter pauses with a card halfway to the pile. "That sucks."

"Yeah," I say. "It does."

He drops the card and leans back in his chair.

"You scared?" he asks.

The question is too direct. Too clean.

I hesitate. Then I nod once.

Carter doesn't react like it's dramatic. He doesn't say "me too" like he's trying to bond. He just looks at me like he's considering something.

Then he says, "You want to know a secret?"

I glance up. "Sure."

He lowers his voice like Patch might be listening from across the room.

"I'm scared all the time," he whispers.

My heart skips a beat.

Carter shrugs like that's just information.

"But I don't let it control me," he adds.

I blink. "What?"

He taps the table with two fingers. "It can accompany me. Whatever." He lifts his chin. "But it doesn't get to be in charge."

I stare at him for a second, not sure what to do with that.

He studies my face, then adds, "I mean, it tries. A lot."

"Then how do you stop it?" I ask before I can stop myself.

Carter's eyes flick toward the doorway, toward the hallway beyond the Commons. Toward the rest of the hospital.

Then he looks back at me.

"I pick something," he says simply.

"Something?" I repeat.

He nods. "Something that keeps me here."

The words hit harder than they should.

"Like what?" I ask.

Carter's mouth twists like he's trying not to smile.

"My mom," he says. "She thinks she's hiding it, but she cries in the bathroom. Like… every day." He looks down at the cards, shuffling them again even though the game isn't over. "And my little sister. She's six. She keeps making me these stupid drawings."

"What kind?" I ask.

"Me with laser eyes," he says, dead serious. "Me punching a dragon. Me playing baseball even though I've never played baseball in my life."

That makes me laugh. A real one. It catches me off guard.

Carter smiles like he won something.

"She doesn't know how bad it is," he says quietly. "But she knows I'm sick. And she still thinks I'm… me." His voice dips lower. "So, I try to be."

I don't know what to say to that.

Carter shrugs again, like he's done being deep.

"And also," he adds, sliding me two cards with a grin, "I like winning."

I look down at the cards. "You're still losing."

"Not for long," he says.

We finish the game. He beats me by one card and acts like he just won the Super Bowl.

Patch wanders over, hands in his pockets.

"Well?" he asks, glancing between us. "Are we making friends or causing emotional damage?"

"Both," Carter says immediately.

Patch laughs. "That tracks."

Carter stands, pushing his chair in. He reaches for his IV pole like it's nothing, like it's just part of leaving the room.

Before he walks away, he looks back at me.

"Hey, Rett?"

"Yeah?"

Carter lifts his chin once. "Pick something."

Then he turns and disappears into the hallway, the wheels of the IV pole squeaking softly behind him.

I sit there for a second after he's gone, staring at the stack of Uno cards like they might rearrange themselves into an answer.

Patch lowers himself into the chair Carter left behind.

"You okay?" he asks, quieter now.

I nod once, even though I'm not sure what that means anymore.

Patch doesn't push. He just sits with me.

And for the first time in a while, I realize something that feels both terrible and true.

Being alive isn't just something that happens to you.

It's something you choose.

Over and over.

Even here.

When I tell Liz later, about my day. How I am being discharged, and my conversation with Carter. Her smile comes first. "That is amazing," she says.

"I will still come back," I tell her. "Every day."

She nods. Eyes tired. Smile stretching across her face.

"Then I will be here," she says.

That almost breaks me. But I stay steady.

Because now I know how.

Because of Liz.

Chapter 22 – Learning to See Again

The automatic doors slide open and the air outside meets me gently.

It isn't cold the way I expect it to be. Not sharp. Not biting. It is softer. Warmer. Like winter has finally loosened its grip. The kind of air that carries the promise of spring even if it isn't fully here yet. I take a slow breath and feel it settle in my lungs.

Weeks have passed since January. Since I came back through these doors for the second time.

Behind me, the hospital hums the way it always does. Ahead of me, the world waits.

Mom stands close, her hand resting lightly on my arm. Dad lingers a step behind us, giving me space without meaning to. No one rushes me. No one says anything important. We just stand there for a moment and breathe the same air.

Then we walk to the car together.

The drive home feels familiar in a way that surprises me. The streets look the same. The houses. The corner store. The long stretch of road that always seems to take forever. But something in me has shifted. Not fixed. Just adjusted.

When we pull into the driveway, the house looks exactly like it always has. Ordinary. Solid. Waiting.

Inside, the noise hits first.

Voices overlapping. Laughter. The clatter of dishes. Someone calling my name from another room. Aunts. Uncles. Cousins. Grandparents. All of them gathered in one place like they have been holding their breath for weeks and finally let it out at once.

They missed me.

I can see it in the way they look at me. Careful but relieved. Smiling but watching. Like they are memorizing the fact that I am standing here instead of lying in a hospital bed.

No one asks too many questions. They hug me. They tell me they are glad I am home. They hand me food and blankets and sit close without crowding. The house feels full again.

When the gathering finally ends and the last goodbyes fade down the hallway, the quiet that follows feels earned.

I make my way down the hall and into my bedroom.

I close the door behind me and sit on the edge of the bed for a moment, just taking it in. The familiar posters. The scuff on the wall by the light switch. The faint creak in the floorboard I always forget about until I step on it.

I lie back and sink into the mattress.

It is soft and worn and exactly right. My body loosens as the bed gives way beneath me. The mattress wraps around me like it remembers my shape. Like a soft, familiar hug. I pull my pillow close and press my face into it, breathing in the scent of home.

For the first time in a long time, my body rests without bracing for anything.

That night, the house settles around me. Doors close. Lights dim. The low murmur of my parents talking drifts down the hallway and fades. Life does not stop just because I have been gone.

It continues.

School feels almost the same.

The halls look the way they always have. Lockers slam. Shoes squeak against the floor. Voices echo in familiar patterns. Teachers greet me like they used to, some with relief, some with caution, all of them trying not to stare too long.

Friends fall back into step beside me without making a big deal out of it. Conversations pick up where they left off. For stretches of time, I almost forget everything that happened. Almost forget the hospital rooms and the monitors and the fear that once followed me everywhere.

That feels like a small victory.

When the final bell rings, I tell my mom where I am going. She nods and reminds me to be home by curfew. No panic in her voice. No hesitation. Just trust.

I don't disappear anymore.

The hospital doors slide open again, but this time I walk through them on my own terms.

The air inside still smells the same. Clean and faintly artificial. But my chest does not tighten the way it used to. I take a few steps forward and almost run into someone rounding the corner.

"Hey," Patch says, stopping short.

I blink, then smile. "Hey."

He looks at me for a second longer than usual. Not in a clinical way. In a noticing way.

"You look different," he says.

"Different how?" I ask.

"Better," he says after a moment. "Healthier. Like you're standing a little taller."

I shrug, but the words land somewhere warm. "I'm just here to see Liz."

Patch's expression softens. "I figured. She'll be glad you came."

"I'm really glad you two have befriended each other," he says. "It helps to have someone who gets it. Someone who makes a place like this feel less heavy."

I nod. "We help each other."

Patch smiles, small and genuine. "I'll let you get to her."

As he walks away, he adds, "It's good to see you back like this, Rett."

I watch him disappear down the hall, then turn toward the commons.

Liz is curled into her usual spot on the worn-down couch that swallows you the second you sit. One knee is tucked beneath her, the other stretched along the cushions like she has made peace with the shape of the space. A movie plays quietly on the television. It is more background than focus. Just noise to keep the room from feeling empty.

Soft conversation drifts through the commons. Children playing games. Laughter rising and falling. The low hum of people keeping each other company. The space feels lived in, not quiet, not heavy.

She looks up when she sees me and smiles, soft and easy, like this is exactly where we are supposed to be.

I sit beside her and let the couch pull me in. The cushions give way beneath us, worn thin in the places where too many bodies have rested and waited and hoped. For a moment, we just sit there together, sharing the quiet without needing to name it.

We talk for a while.

She tells me stories about home. About meals that lasted too long and nights that never felt rushed. About the kind of evenings where no one was in a hurry to be anywhere else. She talks about small moments from before leukemia took over her life. The kind of memories that sound ordinary until you realize how much they matter. The kind you don't think to miss until they are gone.

I listen and laugh. I let her talk. I just enjoy her presence and the way her voice fills the space between us.

After a while, I notice her energy beginning to fade. Her words slow. Her eyes linger closed a second longer between sentences. I suggest we put a movie on, something familiar, something easy.

We spend the rest of the time like that. Sitting together. Letting the movie play. Letting her rest.

At some point, her head settles against my shoulder. The soft fabric of her yellow daisy covered cap brushes against my cheek. She falls asleep there, breathing slow and steady, like this is a place she trusts.

I stay still.

A soft alarm buzzes in my pocket and pulls me back. I glance at my phone and my chest tightens when I see the time. Almost nine. Curfew on a school night.

I shift to stand and the movement stirs her. She blinks awake, disoriented for a second. When she realizes where she is, her smile fades just slightly. She fell asleep during the movie again.

"I have to go," I say quietly.

She nods like she already knew that. Like it does not change anything.

No promises.

No big goodbyes.

Just a quiet understanding that this isn't an ending. That we will come back to this place. To this couch. To this time that seems to stretch and bend when we are here together.

Outside, the air feels even softer than it did this morning.

Liz once told me that loving life isn't about pretending it is easy or fair. It is about noticing it. The warmth in the air. The way a couch holds you. The comfort of a bed that knows your weight.

I am not cured.

I am not finished.

But I am home. I am learning. I am seeing it all.

Chapter 23 – When Sleep Wouldn't Let Go

Spring didn't arrive the way I expected it to.

It didn't announce itself or make promises. It slipped in quietly, through longer afternoons and the softening light that lingered in the Commons after visiting hours were supposed to end. The sun stayed just a little longer against the windows. The air smelled faintly different, like something had shifted without asking permission.

Liz noticed it before I did.

"It smells like outside again," she said one afternoon, her voice thoughtful as she leaned back into the couch cushions.

I glanced toward the window. "It smells like disinfectant." I said laughing.

She rolled her eyes, but still smiled anyway.

By then, spending time with Liz had become part of my routine. Not something I scheduled or questioned. I just showed up. Sometimes with homework. Sometimes with nothing at all. We watched bad television, shared snacks her parents brought, and talked about everything except the things that scared us most.

She stayed awake longer on the days I was there.

I liked to think that mattered.

That evening, the lights in the Commons were dimmer than usual. The television played quietly, something familiar enough to fade into the background. Liz leaned into my shoulder without asking, her head settling there like it belonged.

I stayed still.

Her breathing slowed, her weight pressing a little heavier against me. I looked down at her, ready to say something teasing about falling asleep again.

Her eyes were closed.

I waited.

The movie I was watching ended. Time felt slippery, like it was moving without checking in first.

"Liz," I said softly. "I should probably head back. It's almost 9."

Nothing.

I nudged her shoulder, careful and gentle. "Hey. You fell asleep."

She didn't stir.

My chest tightened.

"Liz," I said again, louder this time.

Nothing.

I pressed my fingers to her wrist, counting even though I already knew what I would find.

One. Two. Three.

Her pulse was there. Steady. Real.

But she didn't wake.

I had never known how loud a quiet body could feel until that moment.

Something cold settled in my stomach.

"Liz," I said again, my voice sharp now, fear pushing past caution.

Nothing changed.

I stood so fast the room tilted. My heart hammered in my chest as I rushed into the hallway, my shoes squeaking against the floor.

"Help," I called out. "I need help." Panic sounding in my voice.

A nurse looked up from the desk, her expression shifting the moment she saw my face.

"She won't wake up," I said, the words tumbling out too fast. "She was just sleeping and now she won't wake up."

They moved quickly. Calmly. Like this was not new.

They followed me back into the Commons. One of them knelt beside Liz, calling her name, checking her vitals. Another pressed a button on the wall.

I stood frozen, my hands clenched at my sides.

Then they lifted her.

And just like that, she was gone.

The hallway swallowed her whole, her blanket trailing behind as they moved away. I took a step forward without thinking, then stopped. I already knew I couldn't follow.

The couch was empty.

The indentation where she had been didn't disappear right away, and that felt crueler than it should have.

I didn't remember leaving.

I only remembered running.

The night air burned my lungs as I ran the entire way home, my backpack bouncing against my side, my thoughts scattered and sharp. I didn't check the time. I didn't slow down. I just ran until my legs ached and my chest felt like it might split open.

When I burst through the front door, I was crying.

"I'm sorry," I said, breathless and shaking. "I'm sorry I'm late."

My mom stood up from the couch instantly. Hearing the unbridled emotion in my voice.

"What's wrong," she asked.

I could barely get the words out.

"I'm sorry I'm late," I said again. "It's Liz. She wouldn't wake up."

The room went quiet.

My mom crossed the space between us in two steps, pulling me into her arms as my legs finally gave out. I cried into her shoulder, the fear spilling out now that I was no longer holding it alone.

That night, sleep never really came.

I lay awake staring at the ceiling, tossing from one side to the other, my thoughts circling the same place no matter how hard I tried to pull them somewhere else.

Every time I closed my eyes, I saw her on the couch. Still. Quiet. Unmoving.

I checked my phone more times than I could count. No messages. No updates.

Morning came anyway.

I told my mom I was not going to school. She didn't argue. She just nodded and told me to let her know if I needed anything. I spent the morning drifting between the couch and my room, the house too quiet, the hours stretching thin.

By early afternoon, I couldn't sit still anymore.

I grabbed my hoodie and left without a plan beyond one thing.

The hospital.

The Commons was empty when I arrived. The couch where Liz had been the night before looked wrong without her, like it had forgotten its purpose. My chest tightened.

I didn't hesitate after that.

I took the elevator up and walked down the hallway to her room.

507

I stood there for a moment, my hand hovering near the door, then knocked softly.

The door opened, and her mom was standing there.

She didn't say anything at first.

She just stepped forward and wrapped her arms around me, warm and steady, like she had been holding that space open all along. I didn't realize how tightly I was wound until then.

"Thank you," she said quietly when she pulled back. "For being there. For calling for help."

I nodded, my throat tight.

"She is sleeping right now," her mom said. "But you are welcome to come in."

The room was dim; the blinds half closed against the afternoon light. Liz lay curled beneath the blanket; her face relaxed in sleep. I sat in the chair near the bed, careful not to make a sound.

Her mom sat across from me.

Her dad was at work, she explained. She told me how tired Liz had been. How the doctors had said rest was good.

Then she smiled.

"You should know," she said, "she talks about you all the time."

I looked down at my hands.

"She worries about a lot of things," her mom continued. "But when she talks about you, she sounds lighter. Like she is fighting for something again. You have made a difference for her. More than you realize."

Before I could respond, Liz shifted.

Her eyes fluttered open slowly. She blinked once, then twice, orienting herself. Her gaze found her mom first.

Then it slid past her.

And landed on me.

She squinted. "Wow," she said. "You could have at least brought snacks if you were going to stare at me while I sleep."

Relief hit me so fast it almost hurt.

"Good to see you too," I said.

She smiled, then softened. "Thanks for being here," she added.

I didn't trust my voice, so I just nodded.

She closed her eyes again a moment later, already drifting, the room settling back into quiet. I stayed where I was.

Spring break was coming.

Ten days away felt longer than it should have. Longer than anything I could measure. As I sat there, watching her breathe, the thought pressed in again, heavy and quiet.

When I stood to leave, Liz reached for my sleeve, just barely, like she was anchoring herself to something solid.

“Come back,” she said.

“I will,” I promised.

I believed it.

What if time didn’t wait this time?

Chapter 24 – The Weight of Staying

The days start to look the same.

School.
Hospital.
Home.
Sleep.
Repeat.

At first, I think the repetition will wear me down. I expect boredom or frustration or the kind of restlessness that comes from being stuck in the same loop. But instead, the routine steadies me. It gives shape to the weeks slipping toward the cruise date, a way to count time without watching it run out.

I wake up early to get ready for school, because I want the extra minutes to get things ready for the day. I shower, pull on whatever hoodie is closest, and eat breakfast half-awake while my mom watches me over the rim of her coffee mug. She doesn't ask where I'm going anymore. She already knows.

School.

Then Room 507.

School passes in chunks. Classes blur together. Teachers talk. I take notes. I do just enough to keep up, just enough to keep moving forward. I don't linger in the halls. I don't make plans after school. When the final bell rings, my bag is already on my shoulder.

I head straight for the hospital.

The sliding doors open with the same quiet whoosh every afternoon, and I swear my body relaxes the second I step inside. The smell of antiseptic. The low hum of machines. The soft murmur of voices. It should feel heavy. Instead, it feels familiar.

Liz's room is dim when I arrive most days. The blinds are usually half-closed, sunlight spilling across the floor in thin strips. She's almost always in bed now. The commons are too much for her lately. Too loud. Too bright. Too draining.

I pull a chair up to her bedside and sit like it's where I belong.

Sometimes she's asleep when I get there. When that happens, I don't wake her. I drop my backpack on the floor, pull out my homework, and do it quietly. Math problems. Reading assignments. Busywork that keeps my hands moving while I keep watch.

When she wakes, she smiles like she expected me.

"Hey," she says, her voice soft.

"Hey yourself."

We play Uno on the tray table balanced across her bed. She wins more often than she should. I accuse her of cheating. She accuses me of being dramatic. The cards slap lightly against the plastic surface, a small, normal sound in a room full of beeping machines.

Other days, we watch whatever's on the tiny TV bolted to the wall. Sitcom reruns. Old movies neither of us fully pays attention to. I read to her when her eyes get tired. She listens with them closed, like the words matter more when she doesn't have to look at them.

I learn the rhythm of her energy. The way she fades faster in the afternoons. The signs that she needs to rest even if she won't say it. I learn how to sit in silence without trying to fix anything.

Her parents drift in and out of the room like tides. Her mom brings coffee, often something for us to eat and sits with us, asking about school, about teachers, about whether I've eaten enough. Her dad asks about sports, about whether I've been keeping up with homework, about the cruise like it's something solid to hold onto.

They start including me without realizing it.

"Do you want anything from the cafeteria?"
"Can you grab her charger?"
"Tell us if she looks too tired, okay?"

I nod every time.

I mean it every time.

The days stack up quietly.

Some afternoons, Liz is too exhausted for games or talking. On those days, I just sit. I do homework. I scroll on my phone with the sound off. I stay. Being there feels like doing something, even when I'm doing nothing at all.

She becomes the fixed point of my life.

Not in a dramatic way. Not in a way that feels overwhelming or confusing. Just… steady. Intentional. She's where I want to be after school. Where my mind goes when I'm not there. Where time slows down enough that it doesn't scare me.

It's hard to believe we have only known each other a few short months. I feel like we have been friends our entire lives.

It's hard for me to remember life before Liz.

The cruise date creeps closer.

Twelve days away.
Then eight.
Then four.

I don't talk about me and my family leaving. She doesn't either. But it hangs between us, unspoken and heavy, like a clock we're both pretending not to hear.

One afternoon, as I'm packing up my backpack to go, she reaches out and lightly tugs at my hand.

"You'll still come tomorrow, right?" she asks.

"Of course," I say without hesitation. "I still have 2 more days before we leave."

She nods, satisfied. "Okay." She squeezes my hand and lets hers fall to the bed.

"I promise. I will see you tomorrow." I say.

When I leave the hospital each night, the sky is already dark. I walk home with my heart full and a smile streaking across my face, as I replay the small moments like they're something I need to memorize. The way she laughed when I dropped all the Uno cards. The way her mom thanked me quietly in the hallway. The way her dad clapped a hand on my shoulder like I was a part of their family.

School.
Hospital.
Home.
Repeat.

The weeks all passed like that.

And somewhere between here and healing, without meaning to, Liz becomes the center of my days.

Not because I'm saving her.

Not because she needs me to.

But because sometimes, staying is the most important thing you can do.

And I'm not ready to leave just yet.

That night, I sit on the edge of my bed with my suitcase open on the floor.

It looks wrong there. Too big. Too real. Like proof of something I am trying not to think about.

Ten days.

I run through it in my head again. Ten mornings she will wake up without me sitting in the chair by her bed. Ten afternoons I will not pull a chair closer or shuffle a deck of cards or read to her when her eyes get tired. Ten nights where I will not walk home replaying the sound of her laugh.

The thought sits heavy in my chest.

I tell myself she will be okay. Her parents will be there. The nurses. The doctors. The routine will continue whether I am part of it or not. I know this logically.

Emotionally, it feels like I am abandoning her.

Like I am stepping out of something fragile and hoping it does not break while I am gone.

I worry about what will happen when I am not around to notice when she gets quiet. When she is more tired than usual. When she needs someone to stay even if she does not ask.

I worry she will think I left because it got hard.

I worry that ten days is long enough for things to change.

I close the suitcase and sit back on my bed, staring at the ceiling. I remind myself that this is temporary. That I promised I would see her tomorrow. That I am not gone yet.

But even then, it already feels like I am disappearing.

The ocean is waiting.

The distance is already growing.

And for the first time since this routine began, I wish I could stay.

Chapter 25 – Far from Room 507

The days blur together in a different way on the cruise.

There is sun and movement and noise everywhere. Music spills across open decks. People laugh too loudly, like they are trying to prove something. Plates are stacked high with food I don't recognize but I try anyway, flavors blending together until none of them stand out. The ocean stretches endlessly in every direction, calm and blue and impossibly large, like it has no memory of what is happening anywhere else in the world.

I am having fun. Real fun.

There are moments when I forget everything else. Moments when I laugh without forcing it. When I feel light. Free. Like the version of myself that existed before hospital hallways and schedules and quiet rooms still lives somewhere inside me.

I swim. I eat until I am full and then eat some more. I sleep in later than I have in months. For the first time in a long while, there are no alarms telling me where to be. No bells. No whiteboards. No machines humming softly in the background.

And still, something is missing.

It shows up in the quiet moments. In the pauses between conversations. In the way my chest tightens when the sun starts to set and I realize there is nowhere familiar to go at the end of the day. I long to see her again.

I check my phone more than I should, even though I know there will not be anything there. No messages. No updates. No way to know how she is doing. The routine I built so carefully does not exist out here, and without it, I feel unanchored. Like I stepped away from something fragile and left it exposed.

Ten days feels longer when you are counting them.

One evening, just after dinner, my mom finds me leaning against the railing, staring out at the water. The pink sky reflects off the surface and I can't turn away. The wind presses against my face, warm and steady.

"You having a good time?" she asks.

"Yeah," I say. "I really am."

She watches me for a moment longer than necessary. "But."

I let out a breath I didn't realize I was holding. "I miss Liz."

She nods, like she already knew that was coming.

"I keep thinking about her," I say. "About whether she is okay. If she is more tired than usual. If she is sitting alone."

My mom rests her arms on the railing beside mine. She does not rush to fill the silence.

“I feel guilty,” I admit. “Like I am choosing this when she does not get a choice at all.”

She looks at me then. Really looks at me.

“You didn’t cause what she is going through,” she says gently. “And you didn’t abandon her by taking a break.”

“I know,” I say. “I just don’t like being gone. It feels like I left in the middle of something important.”

“You care about her,” she says. “That isn’t a bad thing.”

I stare at the floor, my jaw tightening. “I am scared things will change while I am gone. Ten days feels like a long time.”

“It can,” she says. “But it can also pass before you know it.”

Her thumb presses lightly against my shoulder. “And she knows you are coming back.”

I nod, even though the reassurance does not fully settle. Knowing something and feeling it are not the same thing.

My mom stays quiet, waiting.

“I didn’t like leaving,” I admit. “Not now.”

She does not interrupt. Her hand stays where it is.

"Because of her?" she asks softly.

I swallow. The answer sits heavy in my chest.

"Yeah," I say. "I know I can't fix anything. I know I am allowed to take a break. But every afternoon, when I am not there, it feels like something might happen. Like I might miss something that matters."

She continues gently squeezing my shoulder with her thumb, just enough to let me know she is listening.

"I care about her more than I expected to," I say. My voice drops. "And I am scared."

She exhales slowly, like she has been holding that breath for me.

"Scared of what?" she asks, though I think she already knows.

"I am scared I am going to lose her." I pause, "I thought I already did. When she wouldn't wake up."

My mom leans closer, her forehead brushing my temple for just a second.

"That is the risk of loving people," she says. "That fear means she matters to you."

"I don't know how to do this," I say. "How to leave and still be present."

She stays beside me. Solid. Unmoving.

"You already are," she says. "Caring does not disappear because you step away for a few days. And neither does what you mean to her."

I nod. This time, it lands a little deeper.

The sun sinks slowly toward the water, the sky softening as it gives in to evening. Orange fades into pink, then into something calmer, something steadier. My mom slips her arm around me, pulling me in without saying a word.

A tear escapes before I can stop it.

She does not wipe it away. She just holds me as the light disappears below the horizon, and for the first time in a while, I let myself stay there.

The remaining four days move faster than I expect. The excitement softens, replaced by something steadier. Anticipation. I stop counting activities and start counting days. I find myself imagining the hospital more than the ship. The sliding doors. The familiar quiet.

Room 507.

By the last night, my bag is already packed.

I lie in bed and stare at the ceiling, listening to the distant hum of the ship. I think about everything I want to tell her. About the ocean. About the food. About how strange it felt to be away from the hospital after building my life around it. About how even surrounded by so much, I never stopped missing the small room with half-closed blinds.

When we finally land, I feel lighter than I have in days. Home looks the same, but I don't. Something in me is already reaching forward, pulling me back toward the routine I didn't know I would miss.

School.

Hospital.

Home.

Bed.

I don't go to the hospital that night. It is too late. Too much travel. Too many hours spent moving instead of arriving.

But tomorrow.

Tomorrow, I will go straight to her.

I will pull a chair up beside her bed and let the world narrow to the space we share.

And I will stay.

As long as she lets me.

Chapter 26 – As Promised

I get to the hospital later than I want to, but earlier than what would count as reasonable.

Ten would have felt too eager. Nine would have felt desperate. So, I wait until just after ten-thirty, pacing the parking lot once before finally heading inside.

I have two gift bags in my hands. One small. One a little bigger. I check them both again in the elevator like something might have changed since the car.

The doors slide shut.

Third floor.
Fourth.
Fifth.

Room 507.

The hallway smells the way it always does. Clean and faintly tired. Like a place that has seen too many people hope for things they cannot control.

Her door is cracked.

I try not to think about how many times I imagined this room while I was gone. About how many versions of her I built in my head, some of them worse than this, some of them already gone. I tell myself she is here. Breathing. Real. But fear does not listen to logic. It only waits.

Liz is asleep.

The room is quiet in that familiar way, not empty, just hushed. Her body is turned slightly on her side, the blanket pulled to her chest. Her breathing is slow and shallow and steady. For a moment I stay where I am, afraid that moving closer will somehow break whatever fragile peace she has found.

She looks different.

Still beautiful. Still Liz. But paler than I remember. Thinner. Like the version of her I left behind softened while I was gone.

I pull the chair to her bedside and sit.

And I stay.

I don't touch her. I don't speak. I just let myself look. At her eyelashes resting against her cheeks. At the faint shadows beneath her eyes. At how small she looks in the bed, like the room is slowly claiming more of her.

I hate that I missed any of this.

Her parents come in quietly a few minutes later, hospital coffee in hand. Her mom smiles when she sees me, that tired warmth that never quite fades. Her dad nods, grateful without saying it.

Her mom hugs me, soft and careful.

"Welcome back," she whispers. "How was the trip?"

"It was… good," I say. "Really good." I glance at Liz. "I just hated being gone."

They understand without needing more.

I hand them the smaller bag. Her mom opens it slowly, like it might be delicate.

Mexican chocolate. A carved wooden heart. Bright woven bracelets. A painted tile with a blue flower. A tiny bottle of vanilla that smells like warmth and sugar. And at the bottom, a simple pocketknife for her dad.

"Just little things," I say. "Stuff that reminded me of you."

Her dad smiles. "You didn't have to do this."

"I wanted to."

Liz stirs.

Just a shift at first. Then a breath that changes.

Her eyes open.

She looks at the ceiling, disoriented, then her gaze drifts until it lands on me.

Her breath catches.

"Rett?"

I am on my feet before I even realize it. "Hey."

"You're back."

"I am."

She stares at me like I might vanish. “You weren’t supposed to be back yet.”

“I couldn’t stay away.”

“You missed me?” she asks quietly.

“Yeah,” I say. “I really did.”

A small, disbelieving smile tugs at her mouth. “Wow. I must be special.”

“You are.”

I lean forward without thinking and press a gentle kiss to her forehead.

The second I do it, I freeze.

“I’m sorry,” I say quickly. “I didn’t think.”

Her smile only grows. “It’s okay,” she says. “I liked it.”

There is a pause.

“Well,” her dad says, standing, “this just got real awkward.”

Liz laughs. “Dad.”

“What?” he says, hands up. “I’m allowed to be uncomfortable.”

He looks at me and gives a small nod.

Not approval.

Permission.

Liz reaches for the bigger bag. "Is that for me?"

"You don't even know what it is."

"I don't care."

Inside is the handmade *paliacate,* a Mexican head wrap I bought at a local vendor on one of our land days on the cruise. Soft cotton. Deep reds and warm yellows. Tiny flowers woven into the fabric like something alive.

Her fingers slow when she touches it.

"It's not from your grandma," I say, suddenly nervous. "But I saw it and—"

"I love it," she says, pressing it to her chest.

Her mom helps her tie it, gently replacing the old one. The new colors brighten her instantly.

Liz looks at me again.

"I missed you too," she says.

And for the first time since I walked back into Room 507, the weight lifts just a little.

Chapter 27 – What I Hope For

The days fall back into their familiar rhythm.

School.
Hospital.
Home.

The schedule no longer feels like something I am surviving. It feels like something I am living inside of. Mornings come and go without the tightness in my chest I used to brace for. I still notice the bell at school when it rings, the way the hallways flood all at once, voices echoing off lockers and tile. But the noise no longer feels like a warning. It is just noise again. Manageable. Temporary.

At the hospital, I fall into patterns without thinking about them. The same entrance. The same elevator button. The same pause outside Room 507 before I go in. The place feels quieter lately, less like a countdown and more like a place people pass through. I am not waiting for something bad to happen every second I am there anymore.

Liz notices.

She teases me about being predictable when I show up at the same time three days in a row. I tell her consistency is underrated. She says I sound eighty. I tell her she is the one with a favorite chair and a favorite blanket. She smiles at that, like she likes being known.

A few days later, I sit across from my psychologist for the first time since the cruise. The room is the same as always. Neutral walls. Soft lighting. A small plant that never seems to grow or die. A clock ticks quietly above her shoulder, loud enough that I notice it now in a way I never did before.

"How have you been?" she asks.

"Good," I say. Then I pause, considering the word. "Actually… really good."

She does not jump in. She waits, pen resting lightly between her fingers.

"I have not had any symptoms," I say. "No episodes. No warning signs."

She nods and makes a note, but she does not smile yet.

"And how does that feel?" she asks.

"Strange," I admit. "Like I keep waiting for something to interrupt it."

She looks up at that.

"But it does not," I add. "At least not so far."

"And what do you think changed?" she asks.

I think about Room 507. About the chair beside Liz's bed that has started to feel like it belongs to me. I think about the way her head tipped against my shoulder the last time she fell asleep, how she didn't apologize, how she just let herself rest like being here had become safe.

"I stopped living in the future," I say. "Or the past. I started paying attention to what is right in front of me."

She nods slightly, encouraging but careful.

"I used to be afraid of losing things before I even had them," I continue. "Every good moment felt temporary. Like I needed to prepare for the worst so it wouldn't catch me off guard."

"And now?" she asks.

"Now I just let them be good," I say. "Liz taught me that. She does not know how long she has with anything, so she notices all of it. Every laugh. Every quiet moment. Every ordinary day."

I don't say she saved me. I don't need to. The truth is quieter than that.

"My anxiety fed the symptoms," I say. "The worrying. The pressure. Once that quieted down, everything else followed."

She leans back slightly, studying me in a way that feels less clinical and more human.

"And when the anxiety shows up now?" she asks.

"It still does," I say. "Just… less loud. And when it does, I know what it is. I don't let it convince me it is something else."

She nods, satisfied.

"If you could hope for something," she says after a moment, "what would it be?"

The question catches me off guard. It feels different from the others. Less about symptoms. More about intention.

I don't answer right away.

"I want her to feel special," I say finally. "Not like a patient. Not like someone everyone is worried about."

She stays quiet, giving the words room.

"I want her to feel like a kid again," I continue. "Just for a little while. One more night where she gets to laugh and forget and enjoy herself."

I swallow, my throat tightening.

"I know she does not have a lot of time," I say. "I am not stupid. I can see that. I see how tired she gets. How some days take more out of her than others. But I don't want her last memories to be hospital rooms and machines and people whispering around her."

My voice steadies as I finish.

"I want to find a way to bring her light back. Even if it is just once."

She does not write anything down this time. She just nods.

"That is a good hope," she says. "A grounded one."

She pauses, then adds, "It also tells me a lot about where you are."

"Is that good?" I ask.

"It is," she says. "It means you are not trying to control the outcome. You are just trying to show up."

She glances at her notes, then back at me.

"Unless something changes," she continues, "I don't think you need to keep coming here."

The words land softer than I expect.

"This can be our last scheduled visit," she adds. "You have built the tools. You are using them. That is the goal."

I nod, surprised by the lack of fear. There is no spike of panic. No sense that I am losing a safety net.

I thought this moment would feel bigger. Louder.

Instead, it feels steady.

Grounded.

When I leave her office, I don't feel like I am being cut loose.

I feel like I have learned how to stand.

And as I walk down the hallway, my mind drifts back to the question she asked me.

To my answer.

I want her to feel special.

The thought stays with me, settling in instead of passing through. It follows me past the waiting room and down the stairs, out into the afternoon light. I don't know how yet. I don't have a plan or a shape for it. Just a feeling. A pull. A quiet determination that starts to hum beneath everything else.

I find myself noticing things differently as I head back toward the hospital. Small things. Ordinary things. The way the air feels warmer in the sun. The sound of someone laughing too loud across the street. A flicker of music from a car passing by.

Ideas surface and disappear just as quickly. Not fully formed. Not ready. Just impressions. Questions. What makes something feel normal. What makes it feel fun. What makes it feel hers.

By the time I reach the entrance, I am already turning it over in my head. Not naming it. Not rushing it. Letting it take its time.

Just beginning.

Chapter 28 – Taking Shape

I'm still thinking about it.

About what it would mean to make her feel special. About how that might look. How it might feel. The thought follows me everywhere, settling into the quiet spaces of my day and refusing to leave.

My mom and I talk about it in fragments. Half-ideas. What-ifs. She offers suggestions carefully, like she doesn't want to push me in the wrong direction. None of them feel wrong exactly.

They just don't feel right.

Late April settles over the school like a held breath.

Windows are cracked open. Lockers slam harder than usual. Teachers stop pretending the year isn't winding down. There's a restlessness in the hallways that has nothing to do with anxiety anymore and everything to do with anticipation. Everyone seems to be counting down to something, even if they won't say what.

I'm walking between classes when I see it.

I don't mean to stop. I just do.

It's taped to the wall near the main hallway, surrounded by other flyers I've learned to ignore. Bright colors. Big lettering. The kind of thing people get excited about without really thinking why.

I don't read it right away.

I just stare.

Something shifts in my chest—not the old tightness, not fear. This feels different. Clear. Sudden. Like a door opening somewhere I didn't realize existed.

My pulse picks up.

I step closer. Still not reading the whole thing. Just enough to know what it represents.

And then it hits me.

Not the details. Not the logistics.

Just the certainty.

This.

The bell rings, sharp and loud, but I don't move. Students rush past me, backpacks brushing my arm, voices overlapping. I barely register them. My thoughts are already racing ahead, colliding, rearranging themselves into something new.

I turn on my heel and start down the hallway.

I don't walk. I don't hesitate.

I run.

The library doors swing open as I crash through them, breath already shallow, heart pounding for a reason that finally feels right. I scan the room once before spotting an empty table near the back.

I drop into the chair and pull my notebook from my bag.

My pen hits the page hard.

I don't worry about neatness. Or order. Or whether any of it makes sense yet. Ideas spill out faster than I can organize them. Words. Arrows. Question marks. Things circled, then crossed out, then rewritten.

Space.
Timing.
People.
Lighting.
Permission.
Energy.
What she'd notice.
What she'd remember.

I flip the page and keep going.

What feels normal.
What feels joyful.
What feels like hers.
What she's missing.
What she still laughs at.

Another page.

I pause only long enough to breathe before writing again. Adjusting. Adding. Refining. The pieces start talking to each other now, forming connections I didn't see at first.

By the time I stop, my hand aches.

I lean back and count the pages.

Three. Then a half.

It isn't a plan yet. Not really.

But it's something.

For the first time since she asked that question—since I named the hope out loud—I can feel it taking shape. Not as an answer. Not as a promise.

But as a beginning.

And this time, I know.

This one is right.

By the time the final bell rings, I'm walking faster than usual, the notebook tucked under my arm like it might disappear if I let go of it.

At home, my mom notices immediately.

"You okay?" she asks as I drop my bag by the door.

"I think I figured something out," I say.

That gets her attention.

Not panic. Not worry. Just focus.

I set the notebook on the kitchen table and flip it open, pages already bent and smudged with ink. She doesn't lean in right away. She waits for me to start, like she knows this needs space before it needs questions.

"I don't know all the details yet," I say. "But I know what it needs to *feel* like."

She nods slowly. "That's usually how the good ideas start."

I slide the notebook closer, tapping the page with my finger. "I'll need help," I add. "Probably more than I can do on my own."

She doesn't hesitate. "Of course you will."

There's no doubt in her voice. No warning. Just certainty.

"I know someone who could help with something like this," she says carefully. "But we'd need permission."

I nod. "Yeah. I figured."

"And space," she adds, glancing at the page. "And timing."

I pick up my pen and write both down, then immediately cross one out and rewrite it bigger.

She smiles faintly at that.

"And people," she continues. "This isn't something you do alone."

"People," I repeat, adding it to the list. Then circling it. Then drawing an arrow to the margin where I start jotting down names—not committing to anything yet, just possibilities.

She watches me for a moment before asking, "Are you going to talk to her parents?"

The question lands heavier than the others.

"They should probably be aware," she says gently. "Not to stop you. Just to know."

"I know," I say. "I wouldn't do anything without them."

She studies my face, like she's checking for hesitation. For doubt. Whatever she's looking for, she doesn't seem to find it.

Instead, she reaches for a pen of her own and flips the notebook to a clean page.

"This," she says, tapping the paper, "is a really good idea."

I look up at her.

She meets my eyes. "Not because it's easy. Because it's thoughtful. Because it's about *her.*"

Something in my chest loosens.

I lean forward and start writing again. Faster this time. Scribbling things out when they don't feel right. Replacing words. Adding notes in the margins. The page fills quickly.

She offers suggestions, but never takes over.

"What would make it feel normal?" she asks.

I write, then cross it out.

"What would make it feel like hers?" she tries again.

That one stays.

"What might be too much?" she adds.

I hesitate, then underline it.

The list grows. Changes. Evolves. By the time we pause, there are arrows everywhere, notes layered on top of each other, entire sections scratched out and rewritten.

It still isn't a plan.

But it's closer.

We sit there a moment longer, looking at the mess of ink between us.

"We'll take it one step at a time," my mom says. "No rushing. No forcing it."

I nod. "I just want to do it right."

She smiles, soft and proud in a way she doesn't try to hide. "I know you do."

She slides the notebook back to me. "Go talk to him. See what doors he can open. We'll figure out the rest together."

By the time I get to the hospital, I'm later than usual.

I don't go to Room 507 yet. I slow my pace, scanning the halls the way I've learned to. I spot Patch near the nurses' station, leaning against the wall with his arms crossed, talking to a kid I don't recognize. He nods as the kid walks away, then notices me.

"You're off schedule," he says.

"I know," I reply. "Can I steal you for a minute?"

"For you?" he says. "Always."

We step into a quiet corner. I pull out the notebook and hand it to him without explanation.

He flips it open, eyes moving carefully over the pages. He doesn't rush. Doesn't interrupt. Every now and then, he hums or raises an eyebrow, like something clicks into place.

"This is big," he says finally.

"It's still a mess," I say.

He smiles. "The good kind."

He turns another page. Then another. "This is just for Liz?"

I shake my head. "No."

"For everyone," I say. "All the kids here who don't get to leave. Who don't get the things everyone else does. They should get to be part of this too."

Patch's expression softens. "Well then," he says, closing the notebook, "now I love it."

"You think it could work?"

"I don't see why it couldn't," he says. "I'll talk to who I need to talk to. See what we can make happen."

He hands the notebook back. "You're doing something good here, kid."

By the time I make it to Room 507, I'm definitely late.

Liz is awake, staring at the TV without really watching it. She looks at the clock, then at me.

"You're late," she says.

"I know."

She squints. "You're never late."

"I had to take care of something first."

"Something important?"

I meet her eyes. I don't lie.

"Yeah," I say. "Something important."

She studies my face for a moment, then nods. "Okay."

I pull the chair up beside her bed and sit.

And for now, that's enough.

Chapter 29 – Before the Music

By Wednesday afternoon, Liz needs both of my hands to get out of bed.

I stand in front of her, feet planted, arms steady while she swings her legs over the edge. She grips my wrists and leans forward, concentrating like the movement itself requires thought now.

“Okay,” I say. “Slow.”

Her feet find the floor. Her knees wobble.

“I’ve got you,” I tell her.

She looks at me like she’s trying to memorize the way my voice sounds.

“I know,” she says, breath tight but smiling anyway.

We stand there longer than we used to. When she’s steady enough, I help her take a few careful steps, her hand anchored in mine, her other pressed against the wall.

“That’s enough,” I say before she can argue.

“You always say that.”

“And you always push too hard,” I say. “We’re even.”

She laughs, but it fades quicker than it used to. I guide her back to the bed and help her sit. Her legs tremble as she pulls the blanket over them.

"You're getting bossy," she says.

"I've always been bossy."

"That isn't true."

"It absolutely is."

She smiles at me like she's storing the sound away.

Thursday looks much the same, only shorter. Fewer steps. More sitting. More rest between movements. I don't say anything about it. Neither does she.

By Friday, I don't try to get her out of bed at all.

I sit beside her instead, our shoulders touching, the TV on but ignored.

"You're being weird," she says.

"How?"

"You haven't made me walk even once."

I glance at her legs, tucked beneath the blanket. "You need to save your energy."

"For what?"

"For tomorrow."

She goes still for a second, like the word carries more weight than it should.

Her eyes narrow. "You're being sneaky."

I smile. "A little."

"Are you going to clue me in?"

"Nope."

She sighs dramatically and lets her head fall back against the pillow. "I hate surprises."

"You're going to like this one."

She studies me for a moment, then nods. "Okay. But if I don't, I'm blaming you."

"That's fair." I admit.

When I step into the hall a few minutes later, her parents are waiting.

Her mom smiles first. Her dad crosses his arms, but his eyes are warm.

"You want to tell us what's happening tomorrow?" her mom asks.

I hesitate just long enough to decide honesty is better than mystery.

"I'm planning something for her," I say. "In the Commons."

Her dad's eyebrows lift. "What kind of something?"

"Something she won't get otherwise."

He nods once.

"What time?" he asks.

"Nine. Saturday morning."

"I'll be there," he says. "What do you need me to do?"

I exhale. "Everything."

On my way out, I stop by the bulletin board near the elevators.

I smooth one of the flyers flat, then pin it up.

Yellow paper. Black letters.

PROM

SATURDAY

COMMONS

No last names. No explanations.

Just a time and a place.

I hang a few more as I walk down the hall. Near the nurses' station. By the game room. Outside the Commons itself.

No one asks me what it's for.

A few kids read it anyway.

Saturday morning, the Commons is still half asleep when we arrive.

The couch sits where it always does. The tables are scattered with puzzles and card decks. The snack bar hums quietly, stocked and waiting.

Patch claps his hands once. "Alright. Let's clear the middle."

Liz's dad grabs one end of the couch. My mom takes the other. Aliza helps Patch stack chairs. I drag tables toward the walls, one by one, until the center of the room opens up.

Yellow streamers come next. Backdrops. Tape and ladders and quiet adjustments.

Music plays low from someone's phone. Just enough to fill the space without defining it.

Kids wander in and out. Some help. Some sit and watch. Most wear hospital gowns. A few lean against IV poles, smiling like being here is enough.

Liz's dad straightens a table and looks at me. "That good?"

"Yeah," I say. "Perfect."

We work for hours, and I never once feel dizzy or tight or unsteady.

I know why I'm doing this.

I'm doing this because Liz won't get a prom.

Because some things are supposed to happen at sixteen.

Because if I can give her one night where she isn't a patient, then it matters.

When I return to her room later that afternoon, I'm wearing a white shirt and tie.

Yellow.

She squints at me. “Why are you dressed like that?”

I shrug. “You’ll have to wait and see.”

She smiles, already tired, already fading.

I sit beside her and take her hand. Her daisy head wrap brushes my sleeve. We stay like that until her breathing evens out and her fingers loosen around mine.

Her mom meets my eyes and whispers, “Thank you.”

I don’t answer. I just tighten my grip on Liz’s hand and stay.

We have time.

The music hasn’t started yet.

And somehow, she knows it’s coming.

Chapter 30 – Ordinary

Liz's mom clears her throat softly.

"Rett," she says. "Could we have a minute?"

I start to stand.

Liz frowns. "Wait—what minute?"

Her mom smiles in a way that doesn't quite answer the question. "Just a quick one."

I hesitate, then step toward the door.

"For what?" Liz asks again, sitting up straighter now. Her eyes flick from me to her mom.

Her mom reaches for the garment bag hanging on the back of the chair. "You'll see."

Liz tilts her head, suspicious.

"This feels like one of those moments where I should be concerned."

I laugh under my breath. "You're safe. I promise."

She points at me. "If you're lying, I'm never trusting you again."

"That seems extreme."

"Then don't lie."

I step into the hallway before I can talk myself into saying more, and the door clicks shut behind me.

A few minutes later, her dad joins me. He doesn't say anything at first. Just leans against the wall beside me, arms crossed.

"She ready?" he asks eventually.

"Almost."

He nods once, like he trusts that.

When the door opens, Liz rolls out in her chair, and for a second I forget how to breathe.

The dress isn't loud. It doesn't sparkle or try too hard. It just fits her. Like it was waiting. Her daisy head wrap stays in place, framing her face the way it always does, but something about tonight makes it feel intentional instead of necessary.

She looks at me, searching my face.

"What is this?" she asks quietly.

I smile. "You'll see."

We stop at the entrance to the Commons.

I don't push her in right away.

She reads the sign first. The yellow paper taped carefully to the wall.

PROM

Her hand flies to her mouth.

"Rett," she says, breathe catching. "You shouldn't have."

"I wanted to," I say. "I wanted you to have it."

Her eyes shine, and she blinks fast like she's trying to keep the moment from spilling over. I wait until she nods, then wheel her forward.

The room doesn't erupt. It doesn't cheer.

It just slowly wakes up.

Kids turn in their chairs. Someone laughs softly. A couple stands and drifts closer to the cleared space in the middle. Yellow streamers sway overhead. Music hums low from the speakers, warm and careful.

Patch stands near the phone, nodding along like he's been doing this his whole life.

Liz stays in her chair for a while, just taking it in. She smiles at everyone. Accepts compliments. Drinks a soda. Eats a handful of popcorn and calls it enough.

More kids arrive. Some dance. Some sway. Some just watch like being here is the whole point.

I spot my parents near the edge of the room. My mom waves when she sees me. My dad stands beside her, hands in his pockets, looking around like he's memorizing everything.

Liz's mom stands a little apart, eyes glassy. When she notices me looking, she presses her lips together and nods.

I don't look away when I feel my chest tighten. I let it happen.

"This is nice," Liz says after a while.

"It is," I agree.

Liz leans back in her chair, listening to the music drift through the room. Her eyes close for a second.

"I always wished they'd play *Ordinary* at prom," she says, almost to herself.

"It's my favorite."

I nod like I'm just acknowledging it, like it doesn't lodge somewhere deep in my chest.

"I forgot to tell you that," she adds. "Sorry."

"It's okay," I say.

I excuse myself a minute later, weaving through the room until I find Patch by the speakers, phone in hand.

"Hey," I say quietly. "Any chance you could queue up *Ordinary*?"

Patch looks at me for half a second, then nods. "Yeah. Give me a few."

I don't tell Liz. I don't want to promise something I can't control.

A couple songs pass. The room keeps moving. People keep dancing. Liz laughs at something one of the kids says beside her, the sound light and surprised, like it still catches her off guard sometimes.

Then the opening notes drift out of the speakers.

Soft. Familiar.

My breath catches before hers does.

Liz's head lifts.

She looks at me like she's not sure she's hearing it right, like the room might be playing a trick on her.

"You didn't," she says.

I smile. "I might have."

Everything else slows after that. The lights. The voices. The way time seems to stretch just enough to hold us inside it.

Liz looks at me. "Will you dance with me?"

I don't hesitate. "Always."

I lock her chair and kneel in front of her, meeting her eyes. "Are you sure?"

She nods. "Help me."

I slide one arm around her waist, steadying her as she stands. She leans into me, lighter than she used to be, but still determined. Still here.

I listen to the lyrics:
Our colors will fade eventually
So, if our time is runnin' out
Day after day
We'll make the mundane our masterpiece
Oh, my, my
Oh, my, my love
I take one look at you
You're takin' me out of the ordinary

The words settle into me in a way I wasn't ready for. Fading colors. Borrowed time. Making something beautiful out of what we're given. It feels too close to be coincidence. Like the song somehow found us instead of the other way around. This isn't some perfect prom story. It's small and fragile and happening in borrowed moments.

But it's ours. And somehow, that makes it more than enough.

We move slowly. Barely more than turning in place. I let her set the pace, adjusting with every small shift. I feel her weight change. I feel her strength fade and return in quiet waves, like she's borrowing it back just long enough.

Around us, the room fills.

Parents step onto the floor. I catch sight of my mom and dad together, my dad's hand awkward at her waist like he's relearning something he forgot he missed. Liz's parents join them, her mom resting her head against her dad's shoulder, eyes closed.

No one rushes us. No one stares.

For a moment, it feels like we've been folded into something bigger. Like this is what the room was waiting for all along.

Liz looks up at me, her eyes steady now. Clear. Like she's decided something.

She lifts a hand to my collar, fingers curling into the fabric, grounding herself, grounding me, and pulls me just close enough.

I forget the room. I forget the music. There is only her.

The kiss is gentle. Unrushed. It lasts a second longer than I expect, like she wants me to understand it before she lets go.

When she leans back, she smiles—soft, certain.

"Thank you," she says quietly. "For making me feel special."

My chest tightens. I try to answer, but nothing comes out the way it should.

So, I just nod, holding her a little closer, hoping she knows that everything I can't say is right there with her.

When the song ends, the room claps softly, like we're afraid to break something.

Liz sinks back into her chair, exhausted but smiling.

"That was worth it," she says.

"It felt ordinary," she adds. "And that made it perfect."

"It was," I say, and mean far more than the words can hold.

By the time we roll back to her room, her eyes are already closed.

I wait outside while her mom helps her change. When I come back in, she's curled beneath the blanket, still in her head wrap, her hand reaching out without opening her eyes.

I take it.

She falls asleep like that. Just breathing. Just here.

I stay.

The night doesn't rush us.

And for once, neither does time.

Chapter 31 – Still Here

The weeks after prom don't arrive like days usually do.

They fold.

School. Hospital. Home. Repeat.

I keep expecting the world to acknowledge what happened—like there should be a banner somewhere, like the hallway should still smell like popcorn, like the word **PROM** should still be taped to a wall in yellow paper and black ink.

But the Commons goes back to being the Commons. The streamers come down. The lights get unplugged. The floor gets filled again with tables and puzzles and the quiet hum of kids trying to forget where they are.

And Liz goes back to being Liz.

Except she doesn't.

Not all the way.

At first, it's small enough that I can pretend it's nothing.

She eats two bites instead of five.

She drinks half her soda and says it's too sweet.

She smiles when I walk in, but the smile takes a second longer to find me.

"Hey," I say one afternoon, dropping my backpack to the floor and sliding into the chair beside her bed.

"Hey," she answers.

Her mom is in the room, flipping through a magazine she's not reading. Her dad is in the hallway, talking quietly with a nurse. Everything is normal. Everything isn't.

A tray sits on the table beside the bed. A sandwich untouched. A carton of milk still sealed.

"You're not hungry?" I ask, like I'm asking if she wants to change the channel.

She shrugs. "Not really."

"You should eat," I say, and immediately regret it.

She looks at me, amused but tired. "You sound like my parents."

"Yeah, well," I say, forcing lightness. "They're usually right."

She picks up one fry between her fingers, studies it like it's a suggestion, then takes the smallest bite.

"There," she says. "Happy?"

I nod. "Ecstatic."

She smiles again, and for a second she looks like herself.

Then her eyelids flutter like they weigh more than they should.

The next week, she sleeps more.

Not dramatic sleep. Not the kind that alarms people.

Just… more.

More drifting. More half-closed eyes. More moments where her voice fades out in the middle of a sentence and she doesn't even realize she stopped talking.

I still come every day after school.

Sometimes she's awake when I arrive, and we play cards or watch something stupid on the tiny TV, and I tell her about school like she cares.

Sometimes she's asleep, and her mom whispers, "She was up earlier," like it matters, like it's proof that she's still here.

I sit anyway.

I learn how to be quiet without feeling useless.

I learn how to keep someone company without needing anything back.

One afternoon I get there and she's asleep so deeply her mouth is slightly open, her head turned toward the window. The daisy head wrap sits loose against her forehead, soft fabric against soft skin.

Her mom is in the chair beside the bed, eyes closed, hands folded like she's praying without words.

I set my backpack down gently and sit. I don't speak.

Minutes pass. Then more.

Her mom opens her eyes and gives me a tired smile. "Sorry," she whispers. "She said she was going to stay awake for you."

"It's okay," I whisper back. "Let her sleep."

Her mom nods, and something in her face tightens like she's trying to hold herself together without falling apart in front of me.

"She had a good night," she adds, voice soft. "After prom. She talked about it for days."

I swallow. "Yeah?"

Her mom nods. "She said you made her feel… normal."

The word hits me harder than it should.

Normal.

Like that's all we were ever trying to do.

I don't have symptoms.

Not once.

Not even on the days when I walk into the room and can tell, before anyone says anything, that she's smaller than she was a week ago. Not even when I see the untouched food and the extra blankets and the way her parents move like they're trying not to startle reality.

My body stays steady.

My hands don't shake.

My chest doesn't tighten.

And the strangest part is that it doesn't feel like effort.

It feels like… purpose.

One day she wakes while I'm there—really wakes, eyes clear enough to lock onto mine.

"You're doing okay," she says.

I blink. "What?"

She gives me a look like I'm slow. "You. You're… you're not doing that thing."

I know what she means without her naming it.

The panic. The dizziness. The disappearing.

I swallow. "I think it's because of you."

She smiles, small and pleased. "Good," she says. "Then keep coming."

Like she's ordering me.

Like it's simple.

I nod. "Always."

The grief starts before anything is gone.

I don't tell anyone that.

I don't say the word. I don't even let myself think it too loudly.

But it shows up in the way I look at her.

In the way I memorize.

The shape of her fingers around mine.

The exact sound of her laugh when it catches her by surprise.

The way she always tries to sit up straighter when I walk in, like she's proving she can.

The way she says my name sometimes, quiet, like she's checking that I'm still there.

I start noticing details like my brain is taking inventory.

As if I can store her somewhere safe if I pay close enough attention.

One evening she's awake when I arrive, but she looks tired in a way that's deeper than sleep. Her eyes follow me across the room, slow.

"You're doing it again," she says.

"Doing what?" I ask, setting my bag down.

She pats the blanket beside her, and I sit closer.

"That face," she says.

"What face?"

"The one you think I don't see."

I try to laugh it off, but it comes out thin. "I don't know what you're talking about."

Liz watches me for a long second, like she's deciding how honest to be.

"You look at me like I'm already gone," she says quietly.

It's like the wind gets knocked out me. My breath stutters.

"I'm not…" I start.

She lifts her hand, stopping me with two fingers. Not strong. Just certain.

"I know," she says. "I know you're not trying to. But you are."

I stare at my hands in my lap, suddenly unable to meet her eyes.

"I don't want you to do that," she adds. "Not yet."

I look up.

Her eyes are bright, but not frantic. Just real.

“I’m still here,” she says. “Okay?”

I nod, once.

“Rett,” she says, softer now, “I’m still here. So *be* here.”

The words land like a command and a gift at the same time.

I reach for her hand. She lets me take it.

“I’m trying,” I whisper.

“I know,” she says. Then her mouth quirks, a faint smile. “You’re just… bad at pretending.”

A laugh slips out of me. Small. Broken at the edges.

“Yeah,” I admit. “I’m pretty bad at it.”

She squeezes my fingers. “It’ll be okay,” she says.

I hate the sentence because it’s too big for what it’s trying to hold.

But when she says it, it doesn’t feel like a prophecy.

It feels like comfort.

It feels like her, taking care of me even now.

A few days later, she sleeps through my entire visit.

Not the kind of sleep where she shifts or stirs.

Just steady breathing, soft and even, like her body has decided what it needs and is taking it.

Her mom sits beside her, watching her chest rise and fall like that motion is the only thing keeping her standing.

I sit in my usual chair and take Liz's hand anyway.

Her fingers are cool at first, then warm as my palm covers hers.

I don't talk.

There's nothing to explain. Nothing to fix. Nothing to argue into existence.

After a while, her eyes open just a sliver. Not fully. Just enough to find me.

"Hey," she whispers, voice barely there.

"Hey," I whisper back.

Her mouth curves, a tiny smile.

Then her eyes close again, and she's gone back under before I can say anything else.

But her hand stays in mine.

Like she meant it.

I sit there until the light outside the window turns soft and gray.

Until the hallway quiets.

Until the room feels like a held breath.

She sleeps.

I stay.

And I let myself love her without trying to outrun what comes next.

Chapter 32 – A Little Longer

I wake to a gentle touch.

A subtle graze across the back of my hand.

Liz has shifted on the bed, her fingers nudging mine as if she wasn't sure whether to wake me. My eyes open halfway. The room is dark except for the soft glow of the monitor and the hallway light slipping through the cracked door. For a moment, I forget where I am. Then the stiffness in my neck reminds me of the chair, the thin blanket pulled up to my chest, the steady hum of machines filling the quiet.

Liz is watching me.

Her head has shifted on the pillow. One hand rests near the edge of the bed, fingers curled, like she considered reaching for me again and stopped halfway.

"I didn't mean to wake you," she whispers.

"It's okay," I say, my voice thick with sleep as I sit forward and rub my face. "I'm here."

I always am now.

Across the room, her parents sleep in their chairs. Her mom's head is tipped back, mouth slightly open. Her dad's arms are crossed, chin tucked to his chest. They look worn down in a way that feels permanent, like rest doesn't really reach them anymore, no matter how long they sit still.

Liz waits until I'm fully awake.

"I'm scared," she says.

The words land harder because of how simply she says them. No warning. No buildup. Just truth.

I lean closer and squeeze her hand, taking her in, struck again by how beautiful she is.

"Of what?" I ask, even though I already know.

She swallows. Her eyes flick toward the ceiling, then back to me.

"Of dying," she says. "Of it hurting. Of it being lonely. Of it just… stopping."

Her voice trembles on the last word. She presses her lips together, like she's embarrassed by how small she sounds.

"I don't want to die," she adds quietly. "I know everyone keeps telling me it's okay to be tired, but I'm not tired of being here."

I rest my head against the edge of the bed and stroke her hand carefully, like it might break if I'm not gentle enough.

"I know," I say.

She squeezes my fingers. Not hard. Just enough to make sure I'm real.

"What if it's just nothing?" she asks. "What if I disappear and everyone else just keeps going to school and work and laughing like I wasn't ever really here?"

Her eyes fill, and this time she doesn't try to stop it. Tears slide down the sides of her face and into her hair. I look into her eyes and reach up, brushing them away with my thumb.

"If something mattered enough to hurt this much," I say slowly, "then it doesn't just disappear when someone leaves this world behind."

She holds my gaze, breathing unevenly.

"You promise?" she whispers.

I shake my head gently.

"I can't promise what happens next," I say. "But I can promise this mattered. You mattered. And that doesn't just stop."

She nods once, like she's placing the words somewhere safe.

For a while, neither of us speaks. The monitor keeps time for us. The room holds its breath.

Then Liz shifts slightly and lifts her hand, brushing her thumb along my wrist. She looks at me differently now; calmer, steadier.

She leans forward and presses her lips to mine.

It's soft. Brief. Warm.

When she pulls back, she rests her forehead against my cheek, and I feel her exhale.

"Thank you," she murmurs.

I don't ask for what.

I stay where I am, holding her hand. Eventually, her breathing evens out. Her eyes drift closed.

I don't move.

Across the room, her parents keep sleeping. The night keeps going. The world stays exactly as it is, just for a little longer.

I lie back in the chair and close my eyes, but sleep doesn't come back for me.

The room feels thinner now. Like something has already begun to loosen, even though nothing has changed yet. I think about the life I had before the hospital, before these nights, and it feels distant—like a version of myself I wouldn't recognize if I passed him in the hallway.

I try not to imagine this room without her in it. I try not to picture the empty bed, the quiet that would follow. My mind goes there anyway.

So, I keep my eyes open. I listen to the machines breathe for her. I stay awake, afraid that if I let go for even a moment, something will slip away without me noticing.

Chapter 33 – Where the Quiet Breaks

Her hand is still warm in mine.

That is the first thing I notice when my eyes open again. Warmth. Skin against skin. The quiet pressure of her fingers resting in my palm like they belong there. Like they always have.

The room is dim, lit mostly by the monitor and the faint spill of light from the hallway. The air smells like clean sheets and hand sanitizer. Machines hum softly, steady and constant, like the hospital is breathing for everyone inside it.

Liz's eyes are closed.

Her face is calm in a way that almost tricks me. The kind of calm that makes you believe in normal things. Sleep. Rest. Morning.

I shift in the chair, careful not to jostle her hand. My neck aches. My legs are stiff. I try to blink the heaviness out of my eyes, but it clings to me anyway.

I should sit up. I should stretch. I should check the clock.

Instead, I stay exactly where I am.

Her parents sleep across the room in their chairs. Her mom's hair has fallen forward, hiding part of her face. Her dad's arms are crossed tight, his chin tucked down.

They don't move. They look like people who have learned how to sleep in pieces.

I look back at Liz.

Her chest rises.

Then it doesn't.

No— it does. It has to.

I stare at her, waiting for the next breath like it's my job.

A second passes.

Maybe she's in a deeper sleep. Maybe she's finally comfortable. Maybe—

My eyelids flutter. My head dips forward, just slightly, like my body is pulling me down without asking permission. I try to fight it, but my thoughts are thick and slow. The quiet wraps around me. The hum of the machines turns into something distant, like ocean noise.

I don't know when I slip.

I don't know how long I'm gone.

When I come back to myself, the room feels the same.

Dim. Still. Quiet.

Her hand is still in mine.

And then the sound happens.

A long, single tone—sharp and unending—fills the room.

For half a second, my brain refuses to understand it. It doesn't belong here. Not in this quiet. Not with her hand still warm in mine.

The monitor flashes. Numbers shift. An alarm begins to pulse beneath the tone, urgent and mechanical, like the room has suddenly learned how to panic.

Liz's dad jerks awake.

"What—" he says, already on his feet, his chair scraping loudly across the floor. He crosses the room in two steps and grips Liz's shoulder, shaking it once, then again. "Liz?" His voice cracks immediately. "Hey—Liz. Wake up."

Her mom is awake now too, her breath hitching as she stumbles forward.

"Liz," she sobs, saying her name over and over like it might pull her back. "Liz, please. Please."

I turn my head toward her.

She hasn't moved.

Her face is the same calm.

Too calm.

"No," I whisper, but the word doesn't even sound like my voice. It comes out thin, like air.

The door flies open.

Shoes hit the floor hard. Voices cut through the room, fast and sharp.

"Code"

"Vitals"

"Clear the bed"

Someone gently but firmly guides her dad back. Her mom is crying openly now, her hands covering her mouth as she's pulled aside. The room fills with bodies and motion and sound, all of it colliding at once.

Hands move over Liz. Around her. Above her.

I'm still holding her hand.

I don't realize it until a nurse touches my wrist.

"Honey," she says quickly, not unkind, but urgent. "I need you to let go."

I don't.

I can't.

Her fingers feel like the last thing tethering me to the world. If I let go, I don't know what happens. If I let go, it becomes real.

"Rett." Someone says my name, louder now. "Rett."

I blink, and my vision swims.

The tone keeps going.

I finally loosen my grip. Her hand slips from mine, light as paper. I don't even feel it leave until it's gone.

They move between me and the bed.

Someone guides me backward. A voice near my ear says, "Step out for me. Just step out."

My feet obey before my brain does.

I stumble into the hallway.

The door swings shut behind me, but the sound still leaks through—voices, alarms, that long tone like a line drawn straight through my chest.

I take one step.

Then another.

And then my legs stop working.

I hit the wall with my shoulder and slide down, the way you do when you've been holding yourself up too long and your body finally decides it's done pretending.

The floor is cold through my jeans.

I try to breathe and it feels like there's nothing to breathe into. Like my lungs have forgotten their job.

My hands are empty.

My hand is empty.

My throat tightens so hard it hurts. I open my mouth and nothing comes out. No sound. No scream. Just a broken shape of air.

Liz is gone.

The thought lands without warning, heavy and final.

Liz is…

My chest caves in.

A sob tears out of me then, raw and ugly, like it was hiding somewhere deep and just kicked down the door. I fold forward, pressing my forehead into my hands, but it doesn't help. Nothing helps.

The hallway blurs.

Footsteps approach. Fast at first, then slower, like whoever it is sees me and changes pace.

A shadow drops beside me.

Patch doesn't ask questions.

He just sits down on the floor next to me like it's the most natural thing in the world. Like I didn't just fall apart in front of strangers. Like I'm not bleeding out on the inside.

For a moment, he doesn't say anything at all.

He's close enough that I can feel the heat of him. Close enough that I'm not alone in the shape of my grief.

I shake so hard my teeth click.

Patch reaches out and puts a hand on my back. Not patting. Not pushing. Just there, steady.

"I've got you," he says quietly.

The words split something in me.

I sob again, louder this time, and it feels like my ribs might crack.

Patch stays. His hand doesn't move. His voice doesn't change.

"I'm right here," he says, like I can't hear anything else. Like he knows my brain is breaking and the only thing that matters is a single, solid truth.

I press my palms to my eyes until I see stars.

"I was holding her hand," I manage, the words shredded as they come out. "I was— I was right there."

Patch doesn't correct me.

He doesn't tell me I did everything I could. He doesn't try to build meaning out of the moment.

He just stays on the floor with me.

"That matters," he says.

And I don't know if he means it did, or it still does, or it always will.

I only know I can't stand.

I only know the world just changed shape.

Behind the closed door, the noise shifts—voices lower, footsteps rearrange, the chaos pulling itself into order. The tone stops at some point, but I don't notice when. My body is too busy remembering that her fingers were warm in my palm and now they're not.

Patch's hand remains on my back, steady as a heartbeat.

I stay on the floor, breathing in pieces, staring at my empty hand like it belongs to someone else.

And somewhere inside that room, the night keeps going without her.

Chapter 34 – What the Silence Keeps

The house looks the same.

That's the first thing that feels wrong.

The porch light is on. The front window glows warm against the dark. Someone left their shoes by the door like they always do. For a second, I just stand there, staring at it all, waiting for the world to catch up to what I know.

It doesn't.

I unlock the door and step inside.

The smell of home hits me all at once—laundry detergent, dinner from hours ago, something faintly sweet I can't place. It's familiar in a way that feels almost cruel. My backpack slides off one shoulder and lands on the floor with a dull thud.

"Rett?"

My mom's voice comes from the kitchen.

She appears a second later, wiping her hands on a towel, her face already tight with concern like she knew before she knew. She crosses the room in three quick steps and pulls me into her arms before I can say anything.

She holds me hard.

Not the polite kind of hug. The kind that says she's bracing for impact.

I press my forehead into her shoulder. My mouth opens, but the words don't come out right away. They sit there, heavy and unmoving.

"She's gone," I whisper.

Two words.

That's all it takes.

My mom makes a sound I've never heard before. Not a scream. Not a sob. Something smaller and deeper, like it comes from a place that doesn't usually have language. Her arms tighten around me, and she starts to cry.

"Oh, honey," she says, over and over. "Oh, honey."

My dad is there suddenly too, standing just behind her. He doesn't say anything at first. He just puts a hand on my back, steady and warm, like he's anchoring me to the room.

I don't cry right away.

I feel empty. Hollowed out. Like everything important has already leaked out of me somewhere between the hospital hallway and the front door.

My mom pulls back just enough to look at my face. Her eyes are red. Her mouth trembles.

"Do you want to sit?" she asks gently.

I nod.

She guides me to the couch and sits beside me; her arm still wrapped around my shoulders. My dad lowers himself into the chair across from us, leaning forward with his elbows on his knees.

"Do you want to talk about it?" my dad asks.

I shake my head.

Not yet.

They don't push.

We sit there together in the quiet, the kind that presses in from all sides. The clock on the wall ticks steadily, too loud in the stillness. Somewhere upstairs, a floorboard creaks as the house settles.

I stare at my hands.

They're empty.

I keep expecting to feel her fingers there. The quiet pressure of skin against skin. The warmth. I curl my fingers into my palms, like maybe if I hold them tight enough, I can keep something from slipping away again.

My mom reaches for my hand and laces her fingers through mine.

I let her.

"She wasn't alone," I say suddenly, the words tumbling out before I can stop them. "I was there. I was holding her hand."

My mom nods, tears spilling over again.

"I know," she says. "I know you were."

"She was asleep," I add. "I think. I thought she was."

My dad's jaw tightens, but he doesn't interrupt.

"I don't know when it happened," I say. "I don't know if I missed it."

My mom squeezes my hand.

"You didn't miss anything," she says firmly. "You were there. That's what matters."

I swallow hard.

Patch's voice echoes faintly in my head. *That matters.*

The house creaks again. The refrigerator hums. Life keeps going in all these small, ordinary ways, and it makes my chest ache.

After a while, my mom stands and disappears into the kitchen. She comes back with a glass of water and presses it into my hands.

"Drink," she says.

I take a sip. It tastes like nothing.

"I'm going to make some calls," she says softly. "You don't have to talk to anyone tonight. I'll handle it."

I nod again, grateful and exhausted all at once.

She hesitates, then leans down and presses a kiss to the top of my head.

"We're here," she says. "As long as you need."

When she leaves the room, my dad stays.

He shifts in his chair, then reaches into his pocket and pulls out his phone. He doesn't look at it. He just holds it loosely in his hand.

"If you want company," he says, "I can sit here all night."

I glance up at him.

"Okay," I say.

He nods and settles back, saying nothing more.

I lean into the corner of the couch and let my eyes close. Not to sleep. Just to rest them. The house breathes around me, steady and familiar.

For the first time since the hospital, I let myself feel how far away she is.

And how quiet the world sounds without her in it.

Chapter 35 – What's Left Behind

We arrive before I feel ready.

The car idles in the driveway longer than it needs to. No one rushes me. No one has to. I already know what waits on the other side of the door.

Liz's house is louder than I expected.

Not loud the way a party is loud. Not music and laughter and clinking glasses. It's the quiet kind of noise—soft voices overlapping, floorboards creaking under too many careful steps, someone sniffing back tears in a hallway. The kind of sound people make when they don't know what to do with their hands.

The porch light is on.

It shouldn't matter. It's just a bulb. Just a square of warm light spilling out onto the walkway.

But it does matter, because it looks like any other night.

Because the world keeps doing normal things.

Cars line the street. A few people stand outside, shoulders hunched against the cold, speaking in low voices. When I step up onto the porch, the front door is already open. A woman I recognize—one of Liz's aunts, I think—turns her head and sees me.

Her expression changes immediately. Softens. Breaks in the smallest way.

"Oh, sweetheart," she says, like the words have been waiting there all day.

I nod once, not trusting my voice.

Inside, the house smells like candles and food no one is going to eat. Something warm in the oven. Something sweet on a plate. Grief dressed up like hospitality.

There are coats everywhere. Shoes lined up by the door in uneven rows. A table near the entryway holds stacks of folded programs, a guest book, pens. A framed photo of Liz sits beside them, her smile wide and effortless, like she's mid-laugh.

I stop.

I didn't know she could look like that.

Not because she wasn't beautiful in the hospital—she was. She was always beautiful. But this is different. This Liz is sun and motion. This Liz has two feet on the ground and wind in her hair and energy spilling out of her like it doesn't cost her anything.

I step farther into the living room, and that's when I see them.

Photographs.

More than I can count, arranged along the mantle, on side tables, pinned to boards, propped against picture frames like they were gathered in a rush and set down with shaking hands.

Liz at a soccer field, hair pulled back, cheeks flushed, laughing at something off-camera.

Liz on a swing, her head thrown back, eyes squeezed shut in pure, careless joy.

Liz with frosting on her nose, holding up a cupcake like a trophy.

Liz in a Halloween costume I would have teased her about if I'd known her then.

Liz running. Liz dancing. Liz smiling so hard it looks like it might split her face open with happiness.

A Liz I never met.

A Liz before the hospital. Before the monitors. Before the blankets and the tubes and the careful way everyone moved around her like she might shatter.

I stare until my eyes blur.

I think about the Liz I knew—quiet and brave, sharp and funny, stubborn in the way she refused to let anyone turn her into a tragedy. I think about the way she looked at me when she was afraid, and the way she kissed me like she was saying thank you without needing words.

And then I realize something so sudden it almost steals my breath.

I would have loved this Liz too.

I stand there for a long moment, caught between versions of her, trying to hold two different worlds in my hands, knowing neither one will ever fit.

A voice speaks behind me.

"Rett."

I turn.

Liz's mom stands in the hallway leading toward the kitchen. Her eyes are red, but she's upright. Holding herself together in the way people do when they don't have a choice. Like if she collapses, the whole house might collapse with her.

She walks toward me slowly, like she isn't sure she's allowed to move too fast in a house that now belongs to grief.

When she reaches me, she doesn't say anything at first.

She just wraps her arms around me.

For a second, I can't move. Then my body remembers how to be human, and I hold her back.

She smells like soap and exhaustion.

"Thank you for coming," she whispers into my shoulder.

"I didn't—" My voice breaks on the first word. I swallow. "I wasn't going to not come."

She pulls back, wiping at her face quickly, like she's angry at the tears for making themselves visible.

"I know," she says softly. "I know you wouldn't."

Behind her, Liz's dad stands near the kitchen doorway, talking quietly to someone I don't recognize. He looks up when he sees me. His face tightens, like something inside him twists, but he nods.

I nod back.

It feels like a whole conversation, even though neither of us says a word.

Liz's mom keeps her hand on my arm and guides me farther inside. People notice me and soften. A few step forward to hug me. Someone touches my shoulder gently as they pass.

"We're so glad you were there with her," someone says.

My stomach drops.

I don't know what to do with that sentence.

So, I nod.

I let the room carry me for a while.

There's a small table covered with food in the dining room. Paper plates. Napkins. A pot of something warm. Rolls. A casserole. Brownies. People doing what they know how to do when words aren't enough—feeding each other.

I don't eat.

I stand near the edge of the living room, looking at the photos again. The Liz-before-Liz. The Liz I never got to meet.

The Liz I lost anyway.

After a while, Liz's mom finds me again.

This time, she's holding a few things.

At first, I think it's another program or the guest book, but then I see it's a folded sheet of paper. Not typed. Not printed.

Handwritten.

My breath catches.

She holds it carefully, like it might tear.

"Rett," she says, her voice trembling just slightly. "Liz wanted you to have these. The first is her yellow daisy bandana—the one she wore to the prom at the commons. The second is this." She pauses. "A letter."

I stare at it. My hands don't move.

"She made me promise I'd give it to you," her mom adds.

I take the items carefully. The paper is soft from being folded and unfolded. The edges are worn, like it's been handled more than once. I tuck the bandana gently into my pocket.

I can see a few words where the fold doesn't quite hide them.

My name.

In her handwriting.

The room tilts.

Everything becomes too bright. Too loud. Too close.

"I—" I try to speak, but nothing comes out.

Her mom cups my cheek with her hand, the same way Liz used to when she was trying to bring me back to myself.

"You don't have to read it right now," she says. "Not here. Not in front of anyone. Just… keep it. Okay?"

I nod once.

I don't trust myself to do anything else.

A few minutes later, I find the only quiet place I can—a narrow stretch of hallway near the stairs, tucked out of sight. The noise of the house fades into a muffled hum. Somewhere, someone laughs softly—an awkward, startled sound—and then it disappears again.

I sit on the bottom step and stare at the letter in my hands.

My fingers shake.

Not from panic.

Not from sickness.

From grief.

From the weight of her voice trapped inside paper.

I unfold it slowly.

Rett,

If you're reading this, then I was right about something I didn't want to be right about.

I'm sorry for that.

But I wanted you to have this anyway.

I don't really know how to write serious letters. Every time I tried, it sounded like something from a movie—and you know how bad most of those were. (You still watched them with me. Even the really bad ones. Especially the really bad ones.)

Thank you for that.

Thank you for staying when it would have been easier to leave. For sitting in uncomfortable chairs. For playing Uno even when I kept winning and pretending it was luck. For not treating me like I was fragile, even when I probably was.

Thank you for the quiet. For not always needing to fill it. For listening when I was scared and not trying to fix it.

You made the hospital feel smaller. Less lonely. You made me feel like myself again, not just someone who was sick.

I hope you know how much that mattered to me.

If you're hurting right now, I hate that. I really do. I wish I could reach through this paper and tell you it's going to be okay in a way that actually fixes it.

But I can't.

What I can say is this: you were good to me. And what we had was real. And it counts.

Please don't let this be the thing that stops you. You're meant to keep going. To keep showing up. To keep being exactly who you are, even when it's hard.

Especially when it's hard.

Carry me with you if you want. In small ways. In dumb jokes. In bad movies. In moments when you think of me out of nowhere and it hurts a little.

I'll be there.

Thank you for loving me the way you did.

—*Liz*

I can't breathe.

I read it once.

Then again, slower, like reading it carefully enough might keep her here longer.

My vision blurs halfway through. I wipe at my face and keep going, because stopping feels like letting her go twice.

When I finish, I hold the letter against my chest.

Not dramatic. Not like a movie.

Just because my body doesn't know where else to put it.

For a long moment, I sit there on the stairs while the house continues around me—people moving, murmuring, surviving one minute at a time.

Liz is gone.

But her handwriting is warm in my hands.

And for the first time since the hospital, the emptiness inside me isn't completely silent.

It has a voice.

As long as I have this letter, she's not completely gone.

I fold the paper carefully, lining up the creases the way she left them. I slide it back into the envelope and tuck it into the drawer beside my bed. I don't shut it all the way. Just enough.

I lie back and stare at the ceiling.

Sleep doesn't come.

The house keeps breathing around me—pipes ticking, a door closing softly somewhere down the hall, the low murmur of a television left on too late. Everyone else is moving forward in small ways. Getting water. Sitting. Waiting. Surviving one minute at a time.

I roll onto my side. Then onto my back again.

The quiet presses in.

Eventually, I give up and sit up, the letter's weight still warm in my chest even though it's no longer there. I pad out of my room and down the hallway, careful on the stairs, like sound itself might crack something open.

The living room is dim, lit only by the glow of the TV.

Dad is on the couch.

He's sitting upright, not really watching whatever's on the screen. One arm is draped along the back cushion, the other resting in his lap. The volume is low. Late-night noise meant more to fill space than entertain.

He looks over when he hears me.

"Hey, bud," he says quietly. "You okay?"

I shrug. It's the only answer I have that doesn't feel like lying.

He nods like he understands that answer perfectly.

I hover at the edge of the room for a second, unsure what I'm allowed to do. Sit. Leave. Pretend I was just getting water.

Dad shifts on the couch, making space without saying anything.

I sit on the opposite end, curling in on myself, hands folded tight in my lap. The TV flickers between scenes. Neither of us is paying attention.

For a long moment, neither of us speaks.

"I couldn't sleep either," Dad says eventually. Not as an explanation. Just a fact.

I nod again.

The silence stretches. It's different than the one upstairs. Heavier, but steadier. Like it knows how to hold itself.

"I read the letter," I say, the words quiet in the space between us.

Dad turns his head slightly. "What letter?"

"Liz wrote me one," I say. "Her mom gave it to me this evening."

He nods once, slow. "Yeah?"

"She wrote small," I say. "Like she was trying to fit everything in."

Dad exhales softly. "That sounds like her."

I glance at him. He's staring at the TV, but his eyes aren't focused. He looks older in the dim light. Smaller somehow. Like the day has taken more out of him than he's letting on.

"I don't know what I'm supposed to do with it," I admit. "The letter. I mean."

Dad exhales slowly through his nose. "If you figure that out," he says, "you let me know."

That almost makes me smile.

He shifts, elbows resting on his knees now, hands clasped together.

"I keep thinking I should say something helpful," he says after a while. "Something that sounds like it knows where this is going."

He shakes his head once. "But I don't."

I wait.

"I thought being quiet was the right thing," he continues. "Giving you space. Letting you grieve the way you needed to." He glances over at me then, eyes tired but honest. "I'm not sure if I got that right."

"You stayed," I say.

He nods slowly. "Yeah. I can do that part."

He leans back against the couch.

"I can sit here all night," he adds. "If you want."

The words don't rush me. They don't ask for anything back.

I nod, my throat tight.

He doesn't move.

The TV hums softly. The house settles around us. Minute by minute, nothing changes. And somehow, that's enough.

For the first time since the vigil, I don't feel like I'm waiting for the night to end.

I just sit there.

And Dad stays.

Chapter 36 – The Room That Stayed 507

The hospital still smells the same.

That's the first thing that surprises me when I walk through the sliding doors.

Clean. Sharp. Faintly artificial. Like it's trying to pretend nothing has changed. Like it hasn't watched someone stop breathing.

I stand just inside the entrance, my hands hanging uselessly at my sides, the hum of the building washing over me. Wheels roll past. Someone laughs somewhere down the hall. A nurse calls a name that isn't hers.

I don't know why I came.

Except I do.

My feet start moving before I ask them to. Down the same hallway. Past the same desk. Toward the same elevator. My body remembers the path even if my heart doesn't want to. Once again, the elevator chimes at each floor.

Third floor.

Beep.

Fourth.

Beep.

Fifth.

Beep.

The slide doors open.

Room 507 is down the hall to the right.

I walk slower now.

The closer I get, the heavier everything feels, like the air thickens with every step. I pass other rooms—doors open, doors closed, TVs murmuring, parents sitting in chairs that look too small for their fear.

When I reach her door, it isn't cracked anymore.

It's wide open.

That feels wrong.

Inside, the bed is made.

Not the way it was when she was there. No blankets tangled. No pillow indented by the shape of her head. No daisy head wrap folded near the tray table. Just clean white sheets pulled tight like no one has ever slept there at all.

The chair I used to sit in is gone.

There's a different one in its place.

I stand in the doorway, my hand gripping the frame, because I suddenly don't trust the floor to hold me.

"She was right here," I whisper, though no one is listening.

I can still see it. Her head tipped toward me. Her fingers warm in my palm. The way her chest moved so gently it felt like I had to watch it to make sure it kept going.

Now there's nothing.

Not even the sound of machines.

I step inside.

The room echoes in a way it never did before. Like the silence is bigger now. Like it has space to stretch.

Patch stands near the window.

I don't know how long he's been there.

He turns when he hears me.

"Hey," he says softly, like volume might break something.

"Hey."

Neither of us moves for a second.

"She didn't leave much behind," he says. "Most of her things went with her parents."

I nod, even though I don't really know what I'm nodding at.

Patch gestures to the empty bed. "They'll clean it soon. Someone else will get it."

The idea makes my stomach twist.

Someone else.

A different kid. A different story. A different ending.

"This room still feels like her," I say.

Patch's eyes soften. "Yeah. It does."

We stand there together, looking at nothing.

"I keep thinking she's just… somewhere else," I admit. "Like she went for a test. Or fell asleep in the Commons. Like she'll walk back in any second and call me dramatic for being here."

Patch doesn't smile.

"That makes sense," he says. "Your brain hasn't caught up yet."

"My heart has," I say quietly.

We move down the hall toward the Commons.

The doors are open.

Inside, everything looks the same.

The couches. The TV. The game console. The puzzle on the table that still isn't finished.

Except her chair is empty.

It's stupid that I notice that first.

But I do.

I go to it without thinking and sit down, my body fitting into the space it memorized.

This is where she used to curl up. One knee tucked beneath her. Hands hidden in her sleeves. Head tilted just enough to make me think she might fall asleep any second.

The room keeps going around me.

Kids talk. Someone laughs. A nurse hands out snacks.

Life is happening in here.

Just not for her.

I swallow.

"She loved this place," I say.

Patch nods. "She did."

"She said it made her feel normal."

"It did," he agrees.

I stare at the empty space beside me where she should be.

"I don't know how to do this," I whisper. "How to be here when she's not."

Patch sits down across from me.

"You don't have to know yet," he says. "You just have to keep breathing."

The words don't fix anything.

But they hold me for a second.

I stay in her chair longer than I should.

Long enough for the room to shift. Long enough for the ache to settle somewhere deep and permanent.

When I finally stand, it feels like leaving something behind all over again.

I don't look back.

Because if I do, I'm not sure I'll ever move forward.

And Liz once told me staying mattered.

So, I keep walking.

Even now.

Chapter 37 – The Days That Didn't Move

The week after Liz dies, my body keeps waking me up like nothing has changed.

Not because I rested.

Not because I'm ready.

Just because it doesn't know what else to do.

Light slips through the blinds and lands on the wall in a thin yellow line. For a second, I lie there watching it, trying to remember what this light used to mean. School. Hospital. Her.

A weight shifts behind my ribs.

There is no her to go to.

I sit up slowly, like I might break if I move too fast. The room feels unfamiliar in a way that makes no sense. My posters are still on the walls. My clothes are still in the chair where I left them. Everything is exactly where it should be.

And none of it fits.

Down the hall, I hear my mom moving around in the kitchen. The quiet sounds of morning. A cabinet opening. A mug set down. Life starting without asking if I'm ready.

I stay on the bed.

If I go to school, I don't know how to pretend she didn't just die in my hands.

If I don't go to school, I don't know where else to be.

The hospital used to be the place where everything made sense. Where my fear had a shape. Where Liz existed. Where sitting in a chair beside a bed counted as doing something.

Now that place is gone.

I pull on the hoodie I wore yesterday and yesterday before that. The fabric still smells faintly like the hospital. Clean. Soft. Not home.

When I step into the kitchen, my mom looks up immediately.

"Hey," she says gently.

I nod.

She watches me for a second. "Do you want breakfast?"

I shake my head.

"Do you want to go in late today?"

I shrug.

It isn't a decision.

It's an absence of one.

She sets her mug down. "You don't have to go if you don't want to."

"I don't know what to do," I say.

The words surprise me. They come out thin and flat, like they don't belong to me.

My mom nods slowly. "That makes sense."

I lean against the counter, suddenly too tired to stand. "I used to go to school and then I went to Liz. That was the day. That was… everything."

I swallow.

"Now there's just this." I gesture vaguely at the room. "Time."

My mom steps closer, careful. "Do you want to stay home today?"

I think about sitting in a desk. About people asking how I'm doing. About the bell ringing like nothing happened.

"I don't think I can," I say.

So, I don't.

I sit on the couch with my backpack still by the door, the yellow bandana tied to the strap like it's waiting for something that isn't coming anymore.

The house stays quiet.

Around noon, my phone buzzes. A message from a teacher. Something about an assignment. I don't open it.

Another buzz. A friend asking where I am.

I turn the phone face down.

The hours stretch. Not long. Not short. Just… endless. Like time forgot how to move forward.

At some point, I realize I'm holding the bandana in my hands. I don't remember untying it. My fingers worry the fabric, folding and unfolding it, like it's something fragile.

Liz wore this.

That thought hits me out of nowhere, sharp and sudden.

She wore this when she danced with me.

She wore this when she fell asleep holding my hand.

She wore this when she was still alive.

I press it to my face.

It doesn't smell like her anymore. Just fabric. Just thread.

That somehow hurts more.

In the afternoon, I walk outside without really deciding to. The air is warm. Birds make noise like nothing has changed. Cars pass.

The sidewalk leads in two directions.

Toward the school.

Toward the hospital.

I stop at the corner and stand there like I'm waiting for a signal.

My body leans toward the hospital out of habit.

Then I remember.

There is no room 507 to go to.

The building still exists. The bed still exists. The chair I sat in probably still exists.

She doesn't.

I turn away.

I end up walking for a long time with no destination. Past houses. Past trees. Past people who have no idea what just happened to my world.

I don't know what I'm supposed to do with all this time now that she isn't in it.

When I get home, the house is too quiet for the middle of the day.

My mom is on the couch, legs tucked beneath her, hands folded together like she hasn't known what to do with them for a while. The TV is on, but muted. Light flickers across her face without meaning.

She looks up when she hears the door.

For a second, she just stares at me, like she's checking to make sure I'm real. Then she opens her arms without saying anything.

I don't hesitate.

I cross the room and let myself fall into them.

She smells like laundry soap and coffee and something familiar that makes my chest tighten. Her arms wrap around me immediately, firm and certain, like she's afraid if she loosens her grip I might slip through.

"I don't know where to go anymore," I say into her shoulder.

The words come out muffled, but they feel true enough to hurt.

She presses her cheek against the top of my head and holds me tighter.

"We'll figure it out," she says.

Her voice doesn't shake, but I can feel it anyway. In the way her breath catches. In the way her hand keeps rubbing slow circles against my back, like she's trying to convince both of us.

I don't believe her.

Not really.

Everything I thought I knew how to do led me to Liz. To hospital hallways and borrowed couches and quiet afternoons that mattered.

There is no map for this part.

But I let her hold me anyway.

After a while, she pulls back just enough to look at me.

"I don't always know what to say," she admits quietly. "I keep thinking if I find the right words, this will hurt less."

She shakes her head once. "I haven't found them yet."

"That's okay," I say. And I'm surprised to realize I mean it.

She nods, swallowing hard, then opens her arms again. This time, I stay longer.

Tomorrow has nowhere to take me.

And that might be the scariest part of all.

Chapter 38 – The Day That Didn't Fit

The first bell rings, and nothing happens.

Not in the hallway. Not inside me.

Kids move. Lockers slam. Someone laughs too loud near the drinking fountain. A teacher calls out for people to hurry up. All the pieces of school fall into place the way they always do.

I just stand there.

My backpack hangs off one shoulder; the yellow bandana tied to the strap brushing against my side. I feel it every time I breathe. Soft. Real. A quiet weight I didn't choose but don't know how to set down.

I walk anyway.

That's what I do now. I walk because standing still makes the world feel louder.

In first period, I sit in my desk and stare at the board while my teacher writes something about finals and deadlines. The words don't connect to anything. They look like shapes someone forgot to give meaning to.

I open my notebook.

It's blank.

I flip a page.

Still blank.

My hand grips my pencil too tightly. The wood presses into my fingers like I'm holding on for balance instead of writing.

If Liz were here, she would have whispered something sarcastic about how dramatic I look. She would have nudged my elbow just enough to make me smile, even when I didn't feel like I deserved to.

She isn't here.

The room feels wrong because of it. Like someone removed a wall and forgot to tell anyone.

Second period is worse.

People talk. They always do. But their voices don't reach me the same way. They come in muffled, like I'm underwater and everyone else is breathing air.

I try to follow along. I really do.

But every time the clock moves forward, I feel something inside me drift farther away. Not panic. Not fear.

Just absence.

There used to be a next place.

Hospital. Commons. Room 507. Her chair. Her smile. The way she'd look up when I walked in, like the day hadn't really started until I arrived.

Now there's nothing after this.

Just more of this.

By the time lunch comes, my body already feels tired in a way sleep wouldn't fix. I sit at a table with people who know me, who talk to me, who leave space like they're trying not to bump into something fragile.

Someone asks me how I'm doing.

"Okay," I say.

It's a lie that doesn't even try very hard.

I take a bite of my sandwich and chew without tasting it. The cafeteria smells like fries and noise and normal life. It's too much and not enough all at once.

I push the tray away.

The idea of sitting here for three more classes feels impossible. Not dramatic. Just heavy.

I stand.

No one stops me.

The office is quiet when I walk in. The secretary looks up from her computer.

"Everything alright, Rett?"

I think about lying. About saying I feel sick. About giving her something she can write down.

"I just… need to go home," I say.

She studies my face for a second, then nods.

"Go ahead," she says gently.

Outside, the sun is bright and careless. Cars pass. A couple kids cross the parking lot laughing about something I don't hear.

I walk.

Home feels farther away than it should.

When I get there, the house is empty. My mom and dad are at work. The quiet inside is thick, like it's been waiting.

I drop my backpack by the door and go upstairs without taking my shoes off.

My room looks exactly the same.

That's the problem.

I sit on the edge of my bed and stare at the floor. The silence presses against me, filling every space she used to live in.

There is nowhere to go now.

No hospital. No chair beside her bed. No hand to hold.

Just me.

I open the drawer.

The letter is there, folded small. Careful. Like it knows it's important.

My fingers hover over it.

Not yet.

I'm not ready to hear her voice.

But I leave the drawer open.

Just enough.

So, I know it's there.

Chapter 39 – What Still Holds

I sit on the edge of my bed with the drawer open in front of me.

The letter is exactly where I left it. Folded. Careful. Waiting.

For a long moment, I don't touch it. Just looking at it feels like opening something inside me that I barely managed to keep shut all day. School broke me open in ways I wasn't ready for. The noise. The pretending. The way everyone else kept moving like the world hadn't lost its center.

But Liz is here.

In paper. In ink. In the shape of her words.

I pull the letter out and unfold it slowly, like I'm afraid it might tear just from being handled too much.

My name is there again, in her handwriting.

Rett.

It hits me every time. The way she wrote it, slightly slanted, like she was always in motion even when she was sitting still.

I start reading.

I don't rush. I let every line land the way it did the first time. I hear her voice in my head, soft and steady, teasing and kind, brave in the way that wasn't loud.

Thank you for staying when it would have been easier to leave.

My throat tightens.

I think about the chair beside her bed. The way my body learned that space as home. The way being there stopped feeling like something I was doing and started feeling like who I was.

Thank you for the quiet.

I close my eyes.

That was us. Sitting in the Commons. Sitting in her room. Sitting in spaces that didn't need to be filled because we were already there together.

Carry me with you if you want.

My fingers curl around the page.

I already am.

When I finish, I don't fold it back right away. I just hold it, pressed against my chest, like if I keep it close enough it might start to feel like her again.

Eventually, I lay it carefully on the bed beside me and reach for the remote.

The TV hums to life, filling the room with light and sound that feels safer than silence right now.

I scroll until I find it.

Bridge to Terabithia.

Liz loved this movie. Not because it was happy. Because it was honest. Because it understood that loving someone and losing them doesn't cancel each other out.

I press play.

Jesse's world unfolds on the screen. The woods. The rope swing. The secret place that belongs only to him and Leslie.

I don't cry when Leslie dies.

Not right away.

I've already done that part.

What gets me is what comes after.

The way Jesse walks through the world like something essential has been taken from him. The way everything feels hollow and wrong and too loud. The way he keeps expecting her to be there.

That's me.

But then something shifts.

Not quickly. Not cleanly.

He goes back.

He builds the bridge.

He brings someone new into the space they shared.

Not to replace her.

To honor her.

My breath stutters as I watch it happen.

Liz didn't tell me to forget her.

She told me to carry her.

To let her live in small ways. In dumb jokes. In bad movies. In moments that still hurt because they mattered.

The movie ends quietly.

The screen goes dark.

My room feels different now. Not lighter. Not better.

But steadier.

I pick up the letter again and fold it carefully, like I'm tucking something precious away instead of hiding it.

I slide it back into the drawer.

Not because I'm done with it.

Because I know where it is.

I sit there for a long time, staring at nothing, breathing in the quiet.

I still don't know how to be a person without the hospital. Without Liz's room. Without the place where I mattered in a way that was clear.

But I know this:

She didn't leave me empty.

She left me tethered.

And for now, that is enough to keep me here.

Chapter 40 – A Different Speed

The last two weeks of school feel like a countdown for everyone but me.

The hallways buzz with it—summer plans and pool parties, talk of road trips and lake days and late nights that stretch like they're endless. Teachers loosen up. Assignments get lighter. People walk a little faster, like if they move quickly enough they can push June to the front of the line.

Lockers slam. Laughter echoes. Someone yells across the hallway about a bonfire.

And I move through it all like I'm made of something heavier.

My backpack hangs from one shoulder as I walk, and the yellow daisy bandana tied to the strap bobs against my side with each step. It's the first thing I did when I got home from Liz's house. I didn't think about it. I didn't plan it. I just pulled it from my pocket and tied it there, double-knotted like it mattered that it stayed.

It does.

Sometimes I catch people noticing it. A glance. A pause. Then their eyes move on, like they're not sure if they're allowed to ask.

No one does.

In class, teachers talk about finals and projects like they always do. Notes go up on the board. Pencils scratch across paper. Everything sounds normal, and that's the part that feels wrong.

I stare at the clock more than I should.

Not because I'm excited for summer.

Because summer feels like distance.

If Liz were here, she would have made a comment about how dramatic everyone gets about a calendar. She would have said something sharp and funny, then softened it with a smile, like she always did.

I think about that version of her—the one who existed in my life but not in this building—and the ache settles somewhere deep in my chest.

At lunch, the cafeteria is loud in a careless way. Trays clatter. Someone laughs too hard. A group at the next table is counting down days.

"Ten more," a boy says. "Then I'm free."

I chew without tasting anything.

Free.

The word doesn't mean what it used to.

I sit with people I've known for years, and for the first time, I realize how alone grief can be even in a crowded room. No one says her name. No one brings it up. They talk around me, careful not to look directly at the space they know she occupies in my life.

I don't blame them.

I wouldn't know what to say either.

After the final bell, the sun feels too bright. The parking lot buzzes with movement—cars pulling out, kids shouting goodbyes, teachers carrying boxes they'll pretend not to think about all summer.

Everyone moves like they're headed toward something better.

I walk slower than most.

The bandana brushes against my arm as I move. Soft. Familiar. A quiet reminder that she existed, even if no one here ever knew her.

That night, I sit on my bed with my backpack still on, the bandana hanging loose against the strap. I pull Liz's letter from the drawer where I keep it folded and safe.

I don't open it.

I don't need to.

Just holding it is enough.

Downstairs, my parents move through the kitchen, the sounds of ordinary life drifting down the hall; water running, a cabinet closing, my dad's voice asking my mom where something is.

I let the sounds anchor me.

The days pass anyway.

Two weeks.

Then one.

Then the last day.

Teachers clap. Students cheer. Someone yells, "Summer!" like it's a finish line.

I smile because I know I'm supposed to.

But inside, the feeling is different.

Summer doesn't feel like freedom.

It feels like a long stretch of days where I won't accidentally pass a place she once existed. Where I won't have routines to lean on. Where the quiet might have too much room to grow.

I walk out of the building with the crowd, the sun warm on my face, the bandana fluttering lightly against my backpack.

People talk about what comes next.

And I keep walking too.

Because that's what I do now.

I keep moving.

Even when it hurts.

Even when I wish I could stay in the last moment where she still felt close.

Even when the world keeps going without her.

Chapter 41 – Back in Motion

The hospital looks different in the summer.

Brighter. Quieter. Like it's exhaling after holding its breath for too long.

I hadn't planned on coming back. Not really. But one morning, a week into summer, I wake up with the feeling that something is unfinished. Not heavy. Not urgent. Just present.

So, I go.

The sliding doors open, and the familiar smell hits me—clean and sharp and impossible to forget. For a second, my chest tightens. Not panic. Not fear. Just memory.

I keep walking.

The commons is quieter than it used to be. Fewer kids. Fewer parents pacing. A TV murmurs in the corner, something daytime and forgettable.

Patch is behind the desk, flipping through a chart.

He looks up when he hears my footsteps.

"Well," he says, eyebrows lifting. "Look who survived summer break."

I manage a small smile.

"Barely," I say.

studies me for a second longer than necessary. Not clinical. Just attentive.

"You look taller," he says finally.

"I didn't grow," I say.

"Could've fooled me."

We stand there for a moment, the space between us comfortable in a way that surprises me. I hadn't realized how much of this place had become tied to him—his voice, his steadiness, the way he never tried to be more than what he was.

"I just wanted to say thank you," I say.

Patch blinks once.

"For?" he asks, like he genuinely doesn't know.

"For staying," I say. "For… everything."

He leans back against the counter, arms folding loosely across his chest.

"Rett," he says, "you don't owe me anything."

"I know," I say. "That's not why I'm saying it."

That gives him pause.

He nods once, slow.

"Okay," he says. "Then you're welcome."

No speech. No lesson. No attempt to wrap it up neatly.

Just that.

"How are you holding up?" he asks.

I think about the answer.

"Some days are better," I say. "Some days aren't."

"That sounds about right."

I watch him for a second longer than I mean to.

The way he doesn't rush to fill the space. The way he lets the words sit without trying to smooth them over.

And something shifts.

He isn't calm because this place doesn't affect him.

He's calm because it does.

Because he's learned how to stand in rooms like this without trying to fix them. Without needing answers that don't exist.

I think about his sister. About the way he never talks about her unless you ask. About the careful distance he keeps between himself and certain memories.

And for the first time, I understand that silence isn't absence.

It's survival.

I glance toward the commons, half-expecting to see Liz's chair, the spot she always claimed like it was hers by right.

It isn't there.

And that's okay.

"I'm back at practice," I say.

Patch's eyes flick back to me, sharper now.

"And?" he asks.

"And I didn't pass out," I say.

He smiles.

A real one.

"Good," he says. "I had faith in you."

"I didn't," I admit.

"That's usually how it works."

We talk for a few more minutes—nothing important, nothing heavy. Then I head for the doors.

As they slide open, Patch calls after me.

"Hey, Rett."

I turn.

"You ever need anything," he says, "you know where to find me."

I nod.

"I know."

Outside, the sun is warm on my face. I take a deep breath and keep moving.

I don't go straight home.

I ride my bike down the familiar streets, the hospital shrinking behind me, the road opening up in front of me. The knot in my chest loosens a little with every peddle, like my body recognizes where I'm headed before my brain does.

By the time I get to where I am going, the smell hits me first.

The field smells like summer.

Grass and sweat and sunscreen and something metallic from the goalposts baking in the heat. The sound of cleats on turf echoes across the open space, sharp and rhythmic.

I stand at the edge for a moment; helmet tucked under my arm.

My heart picks up speed.

Not fear.

Anticipation.

Coach blows the whistle, and bodies move. Lines form. Voices shout instructions.

No one stops to look at me.

That helps.

I pull on my helmet and jog onto the field.

The first drill is light. Warm-ups. Stretching. The kind of movement my body knows better than my brain ever did.

I move carefully at first, waiting for something to go wrong.

It doesn't.

My lungs burn, but they don't betray me. My legs ache, but they hold. My vision stays clear.

When contact drills start, my pulse spikes.

This is where it used to happen.

This is where my body turned on me.

I line up anyway.

The snap comes. I move. I collide.

And I stay upright.

The shock of it is almost dizzying—not the hit, but the fact that nothing follows. No darkness. No tilt. No loss of control.

Just breath.

Just presence.

I jog back to the line, chest heaving, sweat dripping down my spine.

Someone claps me on the shoulder.

"Good hit," a teammate says.

I nod, stunned.

By the end of practice, I'm exhausted. The good kind. The earned kind.

I sit on the bench, helmet at my feet, and stare out at the field.

I'm still here.

That realization settles deep, steady and quiet.

That evening, I go across town.

Liz's parents' house looks the same as it did before—trim yard, porch swept clean, a wind chime hanging near the door.

Her mom answers when I knock.

She smiles when she sees me. Not the careful kind. The real one.

"Rett," she says. "Come in."

Inside, the house smells like dinner. Not memorial candles. Not grief disguised as food.

Just dinner.

Her dad is at the table, fiddling with something on his phone. He looks up and nods.

"Hey," he says.

"Hey."

We sit.

They ask about football. I tell them I'm back. Her mom looks relieved. Her dad nods like he expected nothing less.

We talk about ordinary things—the weather, a neighbor's dog, a show Liz used to make fun of relentlessly.

At one point, her mom laughs. She stops herself for half a second, then lets it happen.

No one apologizes.

When I stand to leave, her mom hugs me. Her dad claps me on the shoulder.

"Anytime," her dad says. "You know that, right?"

I nod.

"I know."

Outside, the sky is streaked with orange and pink. The air is warm and still.

I walk to my bike and stand there for a moment, hands resting on the handle bars.

Today didn't fix anything.

Liz is still gone.

But my body didn't fail me.

My world didn't collapse.

And the people who matter are still here.

I think about the letter in my drawer. About how she told me to keep going, even when it hurt. Especially when it hurt.

I hop on my bike and ride away, the road stretching out in front of me.

For the first time in a while, it doesn't scare me.

Chapter 42 – Grounded

The air has changed.

It is still warm, but not generous. The heat rests on my skin for a moment before letting go. Like summer is already practicing leaving.

I walk without a destination that matters. The sky is pale and stretched thin, the sun low enough to soften everything it touches. The neighborhood hums quietly. Sprinklers click on and off. A screen door slams somewhere down the street. A dog barks once, then settles.

Liz used to notice things like this.

She said the small details were anchors. That if you paid attention to what was right in front of you, your mind didn't get to run ahead without you.

I think about that as I walk.

The sidewalk gives way to dirt near the field. The grass is cut low, neat and ready. Empty for now. I stop at the edge, not because I am afraid of it, and not because I am longing for it.

It is just there.

Football exists in my life again. Not as a demand. Not as a promise. Just as something I do. Something I enjoy. Something that no longer has to carry the weight of everything else.

That feels like progress, even if it is quiet.

I keep walking. The breeze lifts through the trees and the branches move together, slow and patient. A leaf drifts down in front of me, green still, but thinning at the edges.

Liz would have liked that one.

She would have said it didn't matter what came next. That being here while it fell was enough.

I slow my steps and let the moment stay small. The sound of my shoes on dirt. The way the air cools as the sun lowers. The way the day loosens its grip without asking permission.

I am here because of her.

Not because she saved me. Not because she fixed what was broken.

Because she taught me how to stay.

I carry her with me now. Not as weight. Not as grief.

As presence.

The days move forward whether I mark them or not. School is close enough to feel. Sixteen is coming, even if I don't say it out loud yet.

For once, I don't rush ahead to meet it.

I walk until the streetlights flicker on and the sky deepens into evening. When I turn back toward home, nothing has changed.

Except me.

And even that change is small enough to miss if you are not paying attention.

By the time I fall asleep, the day has loosened its grip on me.

Tomorrow is already waiting.

Chapter 43 – Almost

The hardest part isn't getting better.

It's trusting that better won't disappear the second I stop paying attention.

The first day I wake up without a headache, I don't tell anyone.

I lie still in bed, staring at the ceiling, merged into the quiet. I wait for the familiar pressure to bloom behind my eyes. The warning spin. The nausea curling in my stomach.

Nothing comes.

I sit up slowly. Carefully. Like my body might punish me for moving too fast.

Still nothing.

The room feels normal. Not sharp. Not tilted. Just… there.

I swing my legs over the edge of the bed and rest my feet on the floor. The carpet is cool against my skin. My head doesn't protest. My vision doesn't blur.

I stay like that for a full minute, breathing.

It feels like a trick.

Down the hall, I hear my parents moving around the kitchen. Cabinets opening. A mug set down too hard. Normal morning sounds that used to feel impossibly far away.

I stand.

My balance holds.

That scares me more than the dizziness ever did.

I make it to the bathroom, brush my teeth, splash water on my face. The mirror shows the same version of me, but something underneath looks… steadier. Less hollow.

I don't smile at my reflection. That feels like tempting fate.

At breakfast, my mom watches me out of the corner of her eye, pretending she isn't counting how many bites I take.

"I might go for a walk later," I say, casual on purpose.

Both of them freeze.

Not obviously. Just enough that I notice.

"Okay," my dad says after a beat. "That sounds good."

My mom nods. "We'll go with you."

I shake my head. "I want to go alone."

The word *alone* sits between us, heavy and fragile.

My mom opens her mouth, then closes it again. "Just around the block," she says carefully.

"Just around the block," I agree.

The door feels heavier than it should when I open it. Cold air brushes my face. The sky is pale and clear, like it hasn't decided what kind of day it wants to be yet.

I step onto the porch.

Nothing happens.

The sidewalk stretches out in front of me, familiar and suddenly intimidating. I walk slowly at first, counting steps without meaning to. Ten. Twenty. Thirty.

My chest tightens—not from pain, but memory.

This is usually where it starts.

But it doesn't.

Halfway down the block, I stop. My heart is beating faster than it needs to be. My palms are damp. The world is steady, but my thoughts aren't.

What if this is borrowed?
What if it comes back?
What if believing in this makes it worse when it leaves?

The thought sits in my chest like a stone.

What if this is borrowed?

What if it comes back?

What if believing in this makes it worse when it leaves?

I stand there a second longer, my breath coming too fast, my hands damp like I'm still bracing for impact.

Then my mind does what it always does when I'm scared.

It goes to her.

Liz.

Not the version of her I saw at the end.

Not the thin, tired version who had to measure her energy like it was something she could run out of.

The first version.

The one who looked at me like I wasn't dying.

Like I wasn't a countdown.

Like I was still worth knowing.

In another life, I would've met her somewhere normal.

I would've seen her in a hallway at school, hair pulled up, backpack slung over one shoulder, laughing like the world wasn't fragile.

I would've bumped into her in the cafeteria and apologized too fast.

I would've watched her roll her eyes at me for being dramatic.

I would've walked her home.

I would've texted her dumb things late at night just to make her laugh.

I would've learned her favorite songs. Her favorite places. Her favorite version of herself.

I would've gotten to know her without hospital walls pressing in around us.

Without machines.

Without time.

And the truth is, I think I would've loved her.

Not the desperate kind.

Not the kind that tries to rewrite what we were.

Just the kind that happens when you get enough days to let someone become part of you.

But we didn't get enough days.

We got stolen time.

Borrowed time.

And we spent it the only way we could.

Trying to survive it.

I swallow hard, staring down the street like it might offer an answer.

It doesn't.

All it offers is quiet.

And the kind of ache that doesn't come from being sick.

It comes from realizing what you would've chosen, if you'd had the chance.

Because I would've chosen her.

Every time.

I take a breath and keep walking.

Not because the fear is gone.

But because she taught me something without even trying.

That being here still matters.

Even when it hurts.

Especially when it hurts.

I turn back toward the house.

Then I stop myself.

Standing there, alone on a quiet street, I realize something uncomfortable.

Dying felt familiar.

Living again doesn't.

I keep walking.

By the time I reach the corner, my legs ache—not sick ache, just unused. My lungs burn slightly. It feels honest. Earned.

When I turn back toward home, nothing has changed.

Except me.

And even that change is small enough to miss if you aren't paying attention.

Chapter 44 – Sweet Sixteen

I wake up before my alarm.

That's the first thing I notice.

Not because of pain.

Not because something is wrong.

Just because my body is awake, and for a moment I don't know what to do with that.

I lie there staring at the ceiling, waiting.

For pressure behind my eyes.

For nausea.

For that familiar tilt, like the world is about to slide off its axis.

Nothing comes.

And somehow, that scares me more than the symptoms ever did.

Because pain made sense.

Pain was proof.

Pain was something I could point to and say, *See? This is real. This is why I'm afraid.*

But this—this quiet—feels like standing on the edge of something and not knowing if it will hold.

I sit up slowly, careful the way I've trained myself to be. My feet touch the floor. The carpet is cool. Ordinary.

My heart is steady.

Too steady.

I stand, and the room doesn't spin.

I take one step.

Then another.

I make it to the doorway before it hits.

Not dizziness.

Not sickness.

Just a sudden rush of heat in my chest, sharp and fast, like my body remembered fear even if it forgot pain.

My palms go damp.

My legs, begin to shake.

I can feel the sweat beginning to form at my hairline.

And for a second, I'm right back there again—back in all the mornings where I woke up and counted symptoms like they were the only things that belonged to me.

I close my eyes and press my hand against the doorframe.

Here it is, my brain whispers.
This is where it starts again.

My stomach flips.

My breath comes too quick.

And I almost do it.

I almost call for my mom.

Almost call for my dad.

Almost crawl back into bed and let the day pass without me.

But then another voice shows up underneath the panic.

Not loud.

Not dramatic.

Just steady.

Liz.

Not the way she sounded when she was sick.

The way she sounded when she was sure.

Don't disappear.

I swallow hard and force my lungs to slow down.

In.

Out.

In.

Out.

The fear doesn't vanish. It doesn't snap off like a switch.

It lingers, stubborn and sharp.

But it doesn't take me with it.

I open my eyes.

The hallway is still there.

The morning light is still coming through the blinds like it always has.

And I am still standing.

That should feel normal.

But it doesn't.

It feels like something I don't quite know how to trust yet.

I walk to the bathroom and turn on the faucet. Cold water runs over my hands. I watch it disappear down the drain, steady and unbothered. When I look up, my reflection is the same.

But something underneath it looks… present.

Like I'm not halfway gone anymore.

My chest tightens again, but this time it isn't panic.

It's grief.

Because for a second, I want to tell her.

I want to walk into the Commons and find her on that couch and say, *it's happening. I'm okay. I'm still here.*

And then reality swings back in.

Fast.

Clean.

She isn't there.

She will never be there again.

I grip the edge of the sink until my knuckles whiten, letting the truth settle where it belongs.

I am still here.

And she isn't.

And I have to learn how to live inside that sentence.

Downstairs, the kitchen is already awake. The light through the windows is soft and early. My mom stands at the counter with a mug of coffee. My dad sits at the table scrolling on his phone. Everything looks ordinary, which somehow makes it feel bigger.

My mom looks up first. "Happy birthday."

My dad smiles. "Sixteen."

The word settles slowly, like it's making sure I'm ready for it.

I nod, like I'm confirming it for myself.

There is no cake yet. No candles. Just cereal, toast, and the quiet understanding that something is coming later. That feels right. I don't need the proof all at once.

"We'll celebrate tonight," my mom says.

I smile.

I believe her.

The day moves easily. School passes without incident. A few friends clap me on the shoulder. Someone shouts "Sweet sixteen" down the hall. I let it land without flinching.

That afternoon, I stand on a quiet sidewalk in front of a house I have never been to.

I know whose it is anyway.

I hesitate before knocking. Liz and I never crossed this boundary together. Our world existed inside the hospital—hallways and rooms and borrowed couches. Visiting hours and quiet conversations.

This place belongs to the life she had outside of that.

The door opens before I can talk myself out of it.

Her mom looks surprised. Not startled. Just momentarily unprepared.

"Oh," she says softly. Then she smiles. "Happy birthday."

Her dad appears behind her, already nodding. "Sixteen. That's a good one."

They let me in. The house is warm. It smells like coffee and something baking. Ordinary in a way that feels careful and kind.

We sit at the kitchen table. No one rushes to speak.

After a moment, her mom disappears down the hall and comes back holding a small box. She sets it in front of me gently.

"She would have wanted you to have this," she says.

Inside is a bracelet. Thin. Worn. Familiar.

I recognize it immediately.

Liz used to twist it around her wrist when she was thinking. When she was tired. When she was trying to stay present.

Her dad watches me, then says, "She loved you."

Simple. Certain.

I nod. "I only knew her for five months," I say. "And it felt like we shared an entire lifetime together."

Her mom reaches across the table and takes my hand. "You did."

When I leave, the sun is already lowering. I fasten the bracelet around my wrist myself. It fits easily. Like it has been waiting.

That evening, after dinner, my mom brings out the cake.

Chocolate. Sixteen candles. My parents stand on either side of the counter, smiling like they have been holding this moment carefully all day.

They sing. Quiet and imperfect. When the last note fades, my mom lights the candles.

For a second, a familiar thought flickers—how uncertain things once felt. How carefully I learned to treat good moments.

I feel it.

And then I let it pass.

I blow out the candles in one breath. Smoke curls upward and disappears.

My parents clap. My mom laughs and wipes at her eyes. My dad rests his hand on my shoulder.

"Sixteen," he says again. "We're proud of you."

They don't explain why.

They don't need to.

That night, I lie in bed with the lights off, the house quiet around me. Sixteen feels settled now, no longer hovering above me like something I have to earn.

I let the day replay itself in small pieces. Breakfast. The visit. My parents' voices. The bracelet warm against my wrist.

My eyes drift to the dresser across the room.

The letter is where I left it. Folded. Safe. Put away.

I don't open it.

I don't need to tonight.

It matters. It always will. But I am not anchored to what she left behind.

When I turn onto my side, my eyes land on my backpack across the room.

It is slumped against the wall where I dropped it earlier. Ordinary. Familiar.

Then I see it.

The strip of yellow fabric tied around the strap.

I tied it there after her memorial.

It is the same fabric she used to wrap around her head. Yellow, soft, patterned with small white daisies. Her favorite. She said they made her feel less like a patient and more like herself.

I remember standing in my room with it in my hands, unsure what to do with something that felt too small to matter and too important to put away. So, I knotted it onto the bag instead. Not carefully. Just tight enough to stay.

Now the daisies are faded. The edges are frayed.

I don't get up to touch it.

I don't need to.

It is already part of how I move through the world.

There was a time when staying was heavier than leaving.

When breathing itself felt like work.

When every day was something I had to convince myself to survive.

Back then, I didn't know how to name it.

I only knew that being alive felt heavy.

Now I do.

It was the weight of staying alive.

Liz was not loud about it.

She didn't beg.

She didn't save me in some dramatic way.

She just stayed.

And in staying, she gave me something to stay for.

She became the weight that kept me here, when everything else felt too light to hold me. The tether when everything inside me wanted to drift away.

I am still here.

And she is, too.

Not because I am holding on.

Because I chose to carry her forward.

I close my eyes.

Tomorrow will come.

And for the first time, I am not afraid to meet it.